RISING AND OTHER STORIES

D0830116

"Gale Massey's astonishing debut collection, *Rising and Other Stories*, explores the themes of race, sexuality, childhood, family, hardship and courage in tough, clear-eyed prose. Girls and women on the edges of society are compassionately rendered as the reader is drawn into a world of small towns and smaller lives with such bare emotion it's hard to look away. These stories are more than enjoyable, they are addictive. Brava to an unusually gifted writer."

—Louise Marburg,
award-winning author of *The Truth About Me*
and *No Diving Allowed*

"Massey's writing twists the hearts out of her characters and leaves them exposed, broken, tender, and pulsing on the page. Be forewarned—your own heart will join them."

—Sandra Gail Lambert,
author of *A Certain Loneliness*

"In *Rising and Other Stories*, Gale Massey's characters spring to life with unparalleled vividness and verve. Mothers and fathers, carpenters and grocers, veterans and police officers, church ladies and inmates, these saints and sinners elbow past tragedy, racing trains and swimming their way through alligator-infested waters. These are stories that will stay with you, haunting and wondrous."

—David James Poissant,
author of *Lake Life* and *The Heaven of Animals*

Bronzeville Books, LLC
269 S. Beverly Drive, #202
Beverly Hills, CA 90212
www.bronzevillebooks.com

Copyright © 2021 Gale Massey

Support copyright, support author's authentic works, and maintain a platform
for the arts.

All rights reserved. No part of this publication may be reproduced, distributed,
or transmitted in any form or by any means, including photocopying, recording,
or other electronic or mechanical methods, without the prior written permission
of the publisher, except in the case of brief quotations embodied in critical
reviews and certain other noncommercial uses permitted by copyright law. For
permission requests, write to the publisher at the address below.

This is a work of fiction. Names, characters, places, and incidents either are the
product of the author's imagination or are used fictitiously, and any resemblance
to actual persons, living or dead, businesses, companies, events, or locales is
entirely coincidental.

Library of Congress Control Number: 2020951817

ISBN 978-1-952427-18-3 (hardcover)
ISBN 978-1-952427-19-0 (paperback)
ISBN 978-1-952427-20-6 (ebook)

First Edition

10 9 8 7 6 5 4 3 2 1

Cover Painting: Jim Gleeson
Book Design: Reggie Pulliam

RISING AND OTHER STORIES

GALE MASSEY

BRONZEVILLE™
— BOOKS —

"Freedom's Just Another Word" is an excerpt from
The Girl from Blind River (2018)

"Long Time Coming" appeared in
Walking the Edge, An Anthology (2016)

"Swimaway" appeared in *Saw Palm Literary Journal* (2020)

"Marked" appeared in *Tampa Bay Noir* (2020)

"Ivy Waters" appeared in *Sabal* (2012)

"The Train Runner" appeared in *Seven Hills Review* (2011),
first place flash fiction, Tallahassee Writers Association,
nominated for a Pushcart Prize

For
Erin Mitchell
Tara Vance
and
Christine Walz

Contents

Glass

Dad was a thin man with a high forehead and a bent nose. He wore a black patch over his left eye and worked as a carpenter at a shop across the railroad tracks. Mama took me there a few times whenever Dad forgot to take his lunch box. The place smelled of sweet earthy sawdust, but blades tearing through the flesh of the pine two-by-fours were loud and terrifying. Dad told me some of the men wore earplugs so that they might still be able to hear when they got old. After I started first grade, I never went back to the carpenter shop, but I remember how Dad always smelled of sawdust when he came home in the evenings.

On days when Mama needed the Ford for grocery shopping or a doctor's appointment, Dad would leave the car with her and arrange a ride with John, the Black man who owned the shop. He and Dad had become friends during their time in the army. Dad served stateside in the VA hospital because having lost an eye in a hunting accident as a boy meant he could only serve in maintenance. John, having been injured overseas, had spent several months on the ward where Dad was a janitor. They spent enough time together to form a bond. Then when John needed a reference for a loan from the bank to open his cabinet shop, Dad had vouched for him and in turn became his first employee.

Dad would grab his lunch pail when the sound of a truck's engine rumbled outside on the street. I could feel the tension come off Mama like a heatwave whenever *those people*, as she called them, came to our side of town. It was a bristle of anger, perhaps imperceptible to anyone but her own flesh and blood, but it changed the way she smelled and as her child, I paid attention to that. Fear gave off a metallic smell, anger smelled like sweat. Happy, though—happy had no smell.

Dad paid no attention to these fluctuations. Nothing about Mama scared him. He saw his ride waiting for him on the street and kissed her cheek.

"It's Friday, Sugarfoot," he said to me before he closed the door behind him. "We'll be on the river by tomorrow noon."

I knew this because we went every Saturday and would have gone on Sundays, too, except there was always church.

This weekend was going to be different, though. I was finally tall enough to learn to fly fish, even though I felt like I already knew how just from having watched him my whole life. He'd told me the week before, when he was standing in the middle of the river in his waders, water rippling over the small stones at his feet, shade from the cypress trees falling in his eyes. Dad's line caught on a branch one too many times, and when thunder clouds gathered on the southern horizon, Dad had called it a day. We were collecting the nets and rods and heading to the car when he patted the top of my head. "Sugarfoot, you've grown another inch. Time to get you your own gear." Until then I had sometimes fished with Mama's rod and reel, but that afternoon we'd stopped at the store on our way home. Tomorrow would be my first official lesson.

Dad was more of a fisherman than a carpenter. Out in the middle of a river, his blind eye was a small annoyance, but it didn't hold him back like in the shop, where his measurements had to be checked and approved before the wood got run through the blade. Dad said he'd rather be judged by the fish in his basket at the end of the day than the time it took him to measure a two-by-four.

By the time I got home from school that Friday, it was four and Mama was talking on the phone with another church lady like she did every afternoon. She had gone to the store and had hamburger patties made and lying out on the counter, salted and covered in wax paper. She would put them on as soon as Dad came through the front door and we'd have an early supper. I went to my room to make sure I had my favorite shorts and swimsuit ready for the morning. We'd be up and on the road by the time the sun came peeking through the rear window of the Ford. Five o'clock came and went, but there was no sign of Dad.

I got the rods down from the brackets in the garage, thinking he would want to pack the car after supper. He liked to do that himself, fitting everything in so that the rods didn't hit anyone's head when the road dipped and curved. Inside the house, Mama was on the phone. She paced, looking out the front window occasionally so she would know as soon as he appeared and turn on the stove.

At six o'clock she came outside. "You seen any sign of him?"

"No, Mama" was all I said. She was worried and I didn't want to upset her with my own fears. Dad hated to be late to anything. He was always checking his watch and herding Mama and me to the car. And the shop always closed a little early on Fridays. I listened harder for John's truck to arrive at the corner, waiting for Dad to show up and let me climb on his shoulders for our evening walk around the yard inspecting the row of maple trees he'd planted the year I was born.

Along the street, other fathers were pulling into their driveways, their kids rushing to carry their lunch pails or tool belts. Before that evening I had never paid attention to how similar the houses on our block were. Dirt driveways, cinder-block houses on small plots, tiny front porches.

Sunset was around eight thirty that night and Dad still had not called or come home. Sometimes the deacons held emergency prayer meetings and maybe Dad had gone there, but he would have come home, washed up, and changed into his good white shirt first.

"Did he say anything about going somewhere after work tonight?" Mama was at the door of my bedroom. I was on the floor playing with a doll my cousin had left after her last visit, and as soon as Mama came to my door, I smelled metal. I shook my head. She had the phone receiver in her hand, the mouthpiece covered. She was talking with her brother about going out to look for Dad. Uncle Bud was a cop, big and round and always smelled like donuts.

Mama took her hand away from the phone and spoke into it. "Well, where would I even look?"

Our town was small, a single red light where the train crossed. A main street with a feedstore, a grocery store, three churches. Dad was a simple man who always came straight home from work. He didn't have many friends outside of church. John should have dropped him off hours ago. Outside of our own backyard and garage, I couldn't think of a single place to go look for Dad.

"No, Bud, I have the car. John picked him up this morning," Mama said into the phone. "I'm not saying that. It's just he was the last person I saw him with."

My skin pricked at the accusatory tone. I sniffed the air. Sweat.

"I don't know where he lives. Somewhere across town, over on the south side."

A half hour later Uncle Bud showed up in his cruiser. Another cop rode shotgun. I followed Mama outside. The blue lights flashed in the night and made it hard to see the face of the person in the backseat, but I knew right away it wasn't Dad.

Uncle Bud got out and walked to the porch. "Is that John?"

Mama stood in the doorframe and lifted her chin. "Yes, that's him. He gave him a ride this morning."

I walked past them and went to the cruiser. John always gave me a lemon drop from his pocket. Ordinarily I would smile and hold out my hand, but I just stood there staring at his busted lip, the blood on the lapel of his shirt, the metal handcuffs around his wrists. He didn't look like the man I remembered.

"Get away from there." Uncle Bud waved his hand at me from the porch. "Go inside."

The blood on John's shirt meant he'd been fighting but that made no sense. Unless he'd been fighting with Dad, but Dad wasn't a fighter. And they were friends. Still, I wondered if Dad was at the hospital right now, or worse, at the morgue. The cop riding shotgun had a welt on his chin and I worried that John might have put it there.

"Have you seen my dad?" I asked through the glass, but John looked away.

It was getting toward midnight. Dad had never been out so late unless he'd been called to sit with a dying member of our congregation. Sometimes he had to do that if the preacher was on vacation. Being out this late meant someone was in a bad way. I hoped it wasn't him.

The streetlight at the corner hummed, and colored our yard and a portion of the street with a yellow haze, but beyond it the night sky was a black dome.

"He'll talk once I get him to the station," Uncle Bud said to Mama.

I motioned for John to roll down the window, wondering why he wouldn't talk now and save them from the trouble of going to the station. John looked out the opposite window. He'd never ignored me before.

Uncle Bud pushed me away from the door. "Don't rile him up, girl. They can be nasty when they're provoked."

I stepped backward and looked around for a bee or a hornet, trying to understand what my uncle meant by *they*. It didn't make sense. Until it did. *They* meant John and the others. The ones that didn't live on our side of town or look like us. They worked in car shops. They had their own churches and schools. Cold fear climbed up my back. What did they have to do with Dad not coming home? And who was John if he was a they?

"I said, go inside." Uncle Bud pushed me toward the porch. I yanked my arm from his grip.

From the darkness at the edge of the yard, a tall silhouetted man walked toward me. I yelped when I saw it was Dad and ran to him. He let me cling to his leg. He would make sense of this. We walked to the end of our driveway before I looked up into his face and jerked backward. His face was different and strange. It took a moment for me to understand. He'd taken off the black patch and inside that socket was a brown glass eye.

Uncle Bud stood at the door of the cruiser. He saw the difference, too, and eyed Dad with suspicion.

Mama ran to us, the smell of sweat and metal coming off her. "I've been worried sick! Where have you been all night?"

"I was at the veteran's hospital. They called me at work and said my eye was ready." He looked inside the back of the cruiser and grabbed the door handle but it was locked.

"Hold on," Uncle Bud said.

Dad kicked the door handle. "What the hell are you doing with John?"

Dad never cursed. I wanted him to smell like always, like sawdust, but tonight, he smelled like the inside of a doctor's office.

Mama stared at his face. "You were at the hospital? All this time?"

"Yes. I wanted to surprise you. I took the bus there after work and missed the last bus coming home. I had to walk."

"Why didn't you call?"

"I did call after I missed the bus, but the line was busy They fitted me for it last month. It didn't cost a thing."

All this time John was sitting in the back of the cruiser, dried blood on his lip. Uncle Bud hooked his thumbs on his belt and said, "Shit. What am I going to do with him?"

He started to get in the cruiser but Dad stepped between him and the door. "Get him out of there. I'll take him home." He kept rubbing the temple next to his new eye, and I could tell it hurt him because the socket wasn't used to it yet. He took out a bottle of aspirin from his lunch pail and swallowed a few with the spit in his mouth.

He tried the handle again. "Come on, Bud. You know he didn't do anything."

Uncle Bud stared into Dad's eyes, darting from one to the other like he couldn't tell which one was new, which one was fake. "How am I going to account to the captain for taking the cruiser out this late?"

"How're you going to account for busting him up?"

"I don't need to account for that. He resisted."

"Just say you were out looking for me. You found me, right? Case closed. Now let him out and get back to your family."

Uncle Bud walked to his partner's side of the cruiser and stooped down to talk it over. The other cop yawned, and finally my uncle opened the back door and removed the handcuffs. John climbed out.

Uncle Bud cut the lights on the cruiser and backed out of the driveway.

Mama went back up toward the house. "You had me worried all night for nothing." She didn't seem to care about the missing patch or the new eye.

Dad yelled at John to wait but John started walking up the street. Dad ran inside to get the car keys. Mama told me to get to bed but I pleaded to go with Dad. She slammed the front door behind us after we went back outside.

We found John a few blocks away, walking toward the tracks. I crawled into the backseat and John got in. We drove through town, past the church and the baseball park, and across the railroad crossing. There were fireflies lighting up in the weeds along the tracks.

Dad offered his handkerchief but John waved it away. He brought out his own, spit on it, and dabbed at the blood on his shirt. "I've been thinking, and I believe you and your wife need a second set of wheels."

Dad nodded. "I guess we do."

"Stop here and let me out," John said. We had stopped at a corner in front of a white clapboard church. The door was open and lights were on inside the church.

"It's late. Don't you want to get home?"

"They'll be waiting for me inside."

"Waiting for you?" Dad asked.

"Yes, praying, maybe singing some hymns."

John started to say something but then he just shook his head and got out. He leaned back through the window. "It isn't something you would understand. But when my people see someone like me get picked up at my own house, word gets around fast. We do what we can to get through the night, to comfort the family."

I could see it because I'd seen it on the television. Cops in cruisers dragging a man out of his house, little kids scared and crying, a wife flailing her empty arms.

It wasn't like Dad to let someone out if there was still a way to go, but he pulled to the curb and stared out the opposite window. He wiped his nose and sniffed. He'd never smelled like anything but sawdust before, but at that moment he smelled like sweat. John walked up the church steps and disappeared inside. He didn't look back or wave or say good night.

Dad rubbed his temple again, then reached into his socket and pulled out the glass eye. He stuck it in his shirt pocket and blew his nose into his handkerchief.

We didn't make it to the river that weekend or even that month. Dad stayed on the couch, tending to the headache brought on by having to adjust to that new glass eye. He called in sick the next week for three days straight and lay on the couch, popping aspirin until they gave him a stomachache. Thursday night Mama told him he had to go to work because we couldn't afford to go a week without rent and grocery money.

Friday morning Dad told Mama she'd have to give him a ride to the shop if she wanted to keep the car for grocery shopping that day. I rode with them so she could drop me off at school on her way back home.

By then Dad had given up on wearing his new eye. His family had not been able to afford one back then but too many years had gone by and his socket had shrunken over the years and the glass one didn't fit right. And it was cold when he went outside in the morning, which caused a momentary shock in his forehead. He was hoping the veteran's hospital could order him a smaller one, but until then he was back to wearing the eye patch.

We got to the train tracks and I picked up my feet as we crossed. Mama had taught me to do that for good luck, but the tracks didn't even seem to register with her that day. There was an empty stretch on the other side that marked where one town ended and the other began. The Main street that ran through each town had similar stores: a barber shop, a dry cleaner, a smoked-fish shack. There was a little white church where Dad and I had dropped off John. The grocery store was called Lockhart's and it had wide windows out front pasted over with ads. I'd seen all this before, but that day everything felt different.

Mama turned right on Seventeenth Avenue South. The carpenter shop was a tall metal building behind the stores on Main. Two bays were open, with the garage doors rolled up into the roof. The saws were already keening and I could smell sawdust. Weeds grew at the edge of the parking lot, tiny grasshoppers clinging to the grassy tops, swaying in a breeze. We stopped in the parking lot and Dad opened the passenger door.

John was in the first bay. When he saw Dad, he waved toward the foreman and the saws went quiet as John came over to us. He pulled off his cap and shook Dad's hand. Then he saw me climbing into the front seat and reached into the pocket of his coveralls.

"Hello, Pink Toe." He offered me the pack of lemon drops.

Mama cleared her throat, which was code for *don't even*. She'd never objected before but now the air inside the car smelled metallic. I knew better but reached for them anyway, felt the slap on my forearm, and the lemon drops fell on the ground.

John stepped back and stuck his hands in his pockets. I felt his sigh from three feet away.

Dad bent over and picked up the pack. He looked at Mama and said, "Honey, don't." After taking a lemon drop out of the pack, he handed it to me through the window. I stuck it in my mouth.

John went back inside the shop.

"Why does he call her Pink Toe?"

"Because she's white. Don't make a big deal over it. He isn't being mean."

"Well, I don't like it."

The saws started up again, so Dad leaned through the window. "I don't know why you think it's okay to act like this. You owe him an apology and you know it."

Dad rarely spoke like that to Mama in front of me. The lemon drop felt like a rock inside my mouth. I spit it out and put it in my pocket for later. Mama's eyes were red. She wiped her nose and backed out of the parking lot.

I knew better than to ask what was wrong, so I just put my hand on her shoulder as we drove back across the tracks toward my school. Maybe I was trying to comfort her, or maybe I was reaching out to be comforted. She pulled the Ford into the drop-off zone and I got out.

"Walk straight home after school," she said.

After watching her drive away, I started sobbing in uncontrollable spasms. An animal fear had gripped my midsection. The school secretary came outside but I had no words for my tears. She led me to the school nurse, who gave me a glass of water and had me lie down on a cot. When she left to call Mama, I got the lemon drop from my pocket and stuck it in my mouth. The clean fruity sugar soothed me. I stared at the tiles on the ceiling and thought about the river and my new rod and reel.

Mama didn't answer the phone, but after an hour I recovered enough to go to class.

That night Dad pulled into our driveway in the shop's old truck. It was beat-up and rusted and the door hinges creaked and popped, but the windows worked and the bed in the back was big enough to carry all our gear plus a tent. Sometimes we skipped church on Sunday mornings and camped overnight. There was never anyone else around and Mama and Dad never fought about things while they were on the river.

Later when I got old enough, Dad taught me to drive in that old truck. We took it out every weekend and Dad drove it to work and back every day until his heart gave out. He was fifty-two and I had already gone off to start my own family in Atlanta.

After that night with Uncle Bud, John had never come to our house again to give Dad a ride, but when Dad passed, Mom called John to come pick up the truck. She'd gone through Dad's wallet and found the receipt he'd kept all those years. John had sold Dad that truck for one dollar. In his will, Dad had asked it be returned to his boss.

At the funeral, John wasn't the only Black man to come pay respects. The entire shop closed that Monday afternoon, and every man Dad had worked with showed up. Some white, some Black, all of them grieving.

Afterward, Mama and I stood on the steps in the bright sunlight outside the church while they loaded Dad's casket into the back of the hearse. The men and congregation watched from a distance. I stood behind Mama smelling the metallic sweat coming off her.

"Take these to him," she said and handed me the keys.

When I got to John, he offered his hand. A carpenter's hand, steady and calloused. I used the handshake to pull him in for a quick hug. His shirt, the skin at the back of his neck. The embrace was brief. I could feel Mama staring at us and he pulled away. It would have to be enough, that one last inhalation of sawdust and lemon drops.

Differences

Her mother rested her hands on either side of her swollen belly like it was a basketball she was about to shoot instead of a baby Angel couldn't care less about meeting.

"Your first trip outside the state, your first road trip without me. I just don't like it." She let her mother kiss her forehead as she held her breath against the smell of the cheap shampoo that always gave her a headache. The woman bought that shampoo every time it went on BOGO at the grocery store. Angel preferred lavender shampoo, but they had always had their differences.

"I spent a week at camp last year," Angel hadn't wanted them to argue before the Branches picked her up, but that smell, mixed with the extra hormones that permeated the air around the woman, was a stink that had been bothering her for nine months. She couldn't wait to get away from it.

"Oh, honey. That was just an hour from here."

Her mother released her and Angel backed up one step. Two steps would alarm the woman but one step gave her a break from the odor. In just a few minutes there would be a mile between them, then another. By the end of the day hundreds of miles would separate her from that stink and the unavoidable event of this baby's arrival.

Every afternoon for a month Angel had punched 9-1-1 into her phone as she walked home from school, expecting to come inside and find her mother sprawled on the laundry room floor covered in watery blood, a pint-sized screeching baby by her side, life draining from her eyes.

The Branch family had invited her to come along on their annual road trip. Going with them would get her away from the baby's arrival so she agreed right off. Lisa Branch was a year younger than her. They met in ballet right after her twin brother was killed by a bus on the first day of the school year. Angel guessed she was his replacement so they wouldn't have to stare at an empty seat for a week.

Neither of the girls liked ballet, Lisa because she hated seeing her short fat body in a tutu, and Angel because the pointe shoes killed her toes. She wanted to take contemporary dance where you go barefoot but the class was full so the teacher bumped her to ballet. That excited her mother, especially when she found a pair of used pointe shoes at a thrift store for three dollars. Every Tuesday and Thursday for the entire school year, Lisa and Angel had pulled on their tights and ribbons and hobbled to the barre with a dozen other girls who acted like they owned the world, and one thin boy who she never talked to. But school finally let out for summer break and since her feet had grown longer over the year, she gave the pointe shoes to Lisa. Next fall she'd be in high school and would try out for volleyball. Her mother was against that until she learned about lucrative scholarships for volleyball stars. No doubt the woman would find a pair of used sneakers at a thrift store over the summer.

"Mom, all the details are on the refrigerator." Her mother had been going over the details for five minutes but Angel wasn't listening anymore. She stared down the road leading out of the treeless subdivision where she had spent her whole life, waiting for the white minivan to appear. Finally, they arrived and her mother fell quiet. Mr. and Mrs. Branch sat in the driver and passenger seats. Lisa waved from the back.

"We'll talk in a week," her mom said for the thousandth time because she just couldn't help repeating herself when she was stressed.

Angel climbed in the back next to Lisa and waved goodbye. Her mother's damp hair clung to her face as she made a sad face. She was acting like she was going to be lonely but that was just to make Angel feel better. There was so much work to do before the baby came and Angel knew her mother couldn't wait to get started.

The third bedroom in the house had been a storage room for years, stacked with boxes and piles of old clothes, an old bike. Last week her mom bought three gallons of paint in various shades of pink, dragged everything out of that room, and crammed it all in the garage. Her mother was a big fan of home improvement shows and when Angel's Dad got home from work, the makeover would begin. And there was that crib that needed to be assembled. The van rounded the corner and the last thing Angel saw was her mom waddling back into the house. The woman couldn't be far from a bathroom for more than ten minutes.

Lisa offered up her bag of gummy bears. Mrs. Branch dabbed at her nose with a handkerchief when they stopped at the 7-Eleven to gas up the minivan. Half the subdivision came here each morning for machine-dispensed lattes. Sometimes, if it was freezing outside, she and her Mom would share one on the way to school, trying to sip it without getting burned as the car lurched through stop signs and over speed bumps.

Lisa pulled a juice box out of the cooler at their feet. "Want one?"

Angel took it, conceding that this week there would be no lattes.

Gas fumes filled the back of the minivan and Angel got a little woozy, but then Mr. Branch started the engine and rolled down the windows. She sipped her juice box and watched dark shapes at her feet go in and out of focus. Fifteen miles outside of town the heat rolled off the earthy horizon and she still had a buzz. Five hundred miles of Route 66 laid between them and the Grand Canyon.

Angel snapped out of the daze when she realized Mrs. Branch was talking.

"Dehydration is the enemy. But don't you worry. We'll fight it with water, juice boxes, and bags of gummy bears."

Indeed. The back of the minivan was stacked to the roof with cases of plastic water bottles. They could stop a forest fire with that much liquid, but she doubted the gummy bears would do much against dehydration.

"A person can die out here in a matter of hours." Lisa parroted her mother. Angel let it go knowing this family had made the same trip last year, a few months before the thing with her brother, and this was probably the same conversation they had last year. That's what families did, they said the same shit to each other over and over as though there was comfort in redundancy.

Lisa pulled out an oversized photography book and flipped through images of the canyon. Yellow sunrises, orange sunsets, starry nights, tourists riding burros, and artsy black-and-white shots of the desert sky. She touched the picture with gummed-up fingers, smearing yellow across the pages.

"Nothing to worry about as long as we keep drinking water." Mrs. Branch turned and smiled briefly. Her face, lined and weary, more beautiful than the jagged landscape.

A road sign outside read there was four hundred miles to the eastern rim. There was nothing much to see. The desert, a few fields of soybean. Now and then a crossroad or a truck stop.

Mr. Branch turned the air conditioning off and rolled down the windows. "Let's give the engine a break, don't want it to overheat out here."

He seemed like the kind of man who carried a calculator and a pencil in his pocket even on vacations. Angel suspected he had been a Boy Scout, maybe even an Eagle Scout. The kind of harmless nerd everyone was surprised to see get married and start a family.

Another hundred miles and the land began to change. Sunlight bounced against the sand, off the boulders and mesas. The sky was too bright and made her squint.

Lisa tried to explain how the Grand Canyon was carved out of the earth over millions of years, her foot wiggling intensely with each new fact. No doubt she was spouting data she'd memorized from her father. Angel imagined the brother in the middle seat, a mini version of the dad, and wondered if they had competed in geographical facts as a road game.

It wasn't a game she wanted to play. The wheels whined loudly on the blacktop. Lisa's cheeks flushed with pink, her head dropped to her chest, her lips parted slightly, and drool slipped from the corner of her mouth and she was out. Angel smirked but the heat seeped into her bones too, and her mind drifted dark.

They got out at a truck stop on Route 66 and Mr. Branch refilled the tank. They were still in Texas but closer to Arizona. Mrs. Branch got out and stretched but her body was the shape of a barrel and didn't really bend. A bag of chips fell from the floorboard and she struggled to pick it up. The pain it caused her darkened her face and Angel saw it as such beautiful sorrow. They stopped at a Circle K for gas. The sun neared the flat horizon and cast orange across the sky. Semis on the highway pummeled the van with blasts of wind.

Lisa shook Angel's arm and got out of the van. "Come see the baby desert tortoises."

They walked to the back of the store, a collector's paradise of packing crates, metal buckets, a dismantled fan. She thought about all the reality shows she'd watched with her mom about hoarding. It was the first time she'd thought about calling home.

A boy with hair the color of sand dunes stood next to a cardboard box. His neck was creased with dirt, his hair was dusty as though he'd never encountered running water.

He lifted the lid of the box. "They're fifty cents apiece."

The turtles were the color of sand and smaller than her fist. Five altogether, falling and climbing over each other to tear at wilted pieces of celery. Lisa watched them with shining eyes.

"They're miracles," she said. She handed the boy two quarters. "You're the same boy as last year, aren't you?"

"Yeah, so what?" He stuck them in the pocket of his overalls.

"You're taller."

He slumped a little. "You want just one?" He picked up a turtle and held it out to her.

"One is all I can afford, but I don't want to touch it."

"You bought it. You better touch it."

"No. I bought its freedom. Take it out back where you found it and set it free."

He shrugged. "I remember you now. Don't you have a brother?"

Angel watched the pain spread across Lisa's face. It wasn't nearly as tragic and beautiful as her mother's.

He picked up the turtle and the three of them walked past the junk and into the desert. The ground had turned the shade of copper. The sun was blindingly low and dropping into a Halloween colored sky. He put the turtle down near a hole on the ground, but it didn't move until the boy pushed it with his shoe until it slid into the opening. Lisa sighed as though she had saved the entire species.

That night, Mr. Branch rented adjoining rooms at the Red Roof Inn. Eye contact was not his thing. He avoided Angel's eyes by staring at her forehead. She wasn't even sure if he knew her name. It creeped her out until she realized it meant she would never have to talk to him. That she wouldn't have to answer the dozens of questions her dad asked every night at the dinner table. She imagined her dad now, painting the nursery, fumbling with the assembly directions for the crib, dropping the screws and swearing under his breath. Mr. Branch disappeared after dinner to clean the windshield and check the pressure in the tires and it was fine that he was gone.

They had all fallen asleep. Lisa flat on her stomach, the door joining the two rooms left slightly ajar. Angel turned the television back on, kept the volume low, and sat in front of it on the floor. She watched all the late night shows her mother prohibited her from seeing and woke up the next morning on the floor. No one knew and it was no one's business.

The second morning on the road she began to understand the freedom it offered. She never wanted to go home. The world was wide. It spread out on both sides of the highway to endless horizons. Something had begun seeping out of her marrow and into her blood. This is the freedom she'd been waiting for her whole life.

Mrs. Branch glanced at the door for her husband who was taking a long time to return from the bathroom. Her confidence slipped. She didn't want to order without him even though when he finally arrived, he would order a BLT, not toasted, with a side of coleslaw, like he always did. She smiled when Angel ordered soup and salad with low-fat Italian dressing instead of Ranch, and unsweetened iced tea instead of cherry Coke. It was the sorrowful smile Angel was beginning to adore. Lisa would only eat hamburgers and French fries and she had grown pudgier in just two days on the road. It confused her how a woman who had the beauty of a pop star had a daughter who seemed so oblivious. Lisa tore at a package of crackers and stuffed them in her mouth.

"A salad, Lisa. Wouldn't you like a salad?" Mrs. Branch asked.

Lisa pouted. She stared at Angel and waited for a sign of solidarity but all Angel gave up was a tight-lipped smile and raised eyebrows.

Back on the road, Lisa brought out a stack of postcards of the canyon. They were in Arizona now, traveling west, into the glaring afternoon sun, and Angel was starving. She opened another bag of gummy bears and picked out all the red ones. It didn't matter. Lisa would only eat the yellow and green ones now because those were the ones her brother liked. When she smiled her mouth was stained yellow. Tethered by their seatbelts, they were enslaved by the whirring noise of the wheels on the highway and the relentless horizon of sand.

They stopped again for gas and gorged on waffle cones. Mrs. Branch got vanilla with chocolate syrup and sprinkles. Angel had taken her more for the pistachio type. Lisa got strawberry in memory of the brother, a fact when spoken aloud made the mother dump her cone in the garbage bin and wait in the car. Mr. Branch shot Lisa a hard look that Angel noted but pretended to ignore.

The sugar sent her sailing between nervous energy and sluggishness. After two days on the road the backseat felt like a cage. She imagined running on the asphalt alongside the car. Every afternoon Mr. Branch worried about overheating the car engine, so the windows were rolled down again. Wind whipped her hair into her eyes. She closed her eyes and imagined her legs pumping down the highway alongside the car.

The entrance to a national park led them to a ridge.

Mr. Branch parked the car and he and Mrs. Branch popped the minivan's hood to stare at the steam coming off the engine. Lisa tore off her seatbelt and picked up a wooden box that had been sitting at her feet. She pushed her pudgy bottom through the guardrails and got stuck, but managed to get to the edge. She put the box on the ground near her feet and stood near the edge with her arms spread wide. Then, very quickly, she grabbed the box and emptied it into the canyon. Dust. Nothing but white powder. It caught for a moment and hung there, suspended for an instant, then falling and falling, like a cloud that was too heavy to float.

Out in the canyon, two condors floated, dipping then climbing, side by side.

"I want to fly like that." Lisa stretched her arms out like a bird, and spun a tight circle at the edge of the cliff. Red rocks jutted at strange angles, shadows from overhead clouds darkened the cliffs. The gorge seemed so empty. Enough room for entire planets.

Lisa stopped spinning in front of Angel, her arms out like a bird, her back to the canyon. "Push me."

Tears rimmed Lisa's eyes. Angel felt a thrill in her belly.

"Do it." Lisa had backed up, her flipflops an inch from the edge. Her face radiant, broken.

Angel touched Lisa's chest and the girl fell backward. "Oh," she whispered with wide eyes. Her body twisted, her arms grabbing at air.

The gorge spread for miles at Angel's feet in shades of red and purple, deepening in shades of blood. Across the miles, condors glided like specks against the lower cliffs. They called out in the distance. One screech, then another, then nothing.

Mrs. Branch called out from the back of the minivan where she was sorting through empty juice boxes. "Lisa, come over here and help." Angel watched as the woman scanned the parking lot but there was no sign of her daughter.

∼

Mr. Branch got Angel's suitcase from the back and set it on the sidewalk by the drop-off lane at the Las Vegas airport. Her flight home was scheduled to depart in an hour; everyone had agreed that under the circumstances, she was old enough to fly without a chaperone. For the first time, Mr. Branch looked at her. His face seemed ancient and wrecked. He searched her eyes as if he would find some answer. Mrs. Branch hadn't spoken at all. They hadn't seen a thing. No one had. Angel stared back, amazed at how thoroughly they had been crushed.

That night, when she got home, her mother was lying on the couch, the baby asleep on her chest. She whispered, "Come see your sister."

The baby's face was tiny, her lips the color of blood, her shriek as loud as a condor.

Lucky Girl

On that last morning I headed toward the deserted, bright beach south of my shack. The sun was high overhead, sitting alone in a vacant sky. I hated to think of its isolation, how lonely it must be as it trudged overhead day after day, cursed with a timeless existence. A small breeze licked at the sweat beads popping up along my upper lip as I walked. The summer had been hot and relentless.

Every night I dreamed of him, as though the dreams would keep him alive. But the dreams were always just more goodbyes, though they always felt as real as that last day. His hand letting go of mine, the skin on his fingers transparent and wasted, the bones so shrunken they could no longer hold his wedding band. But it wasn't really a dream. It was a memory I fell prey to whenever I fell asleep. Every morning when the dream ended, I woke with grief sitting like a heat wave behind my eyes.

The roped bridge connecting the mainland to the island swayed beneath my feet when I passed over the water. The horizon tilted one way and then another. I kept walking toward the stinging saltwater that I would dive into, hoping to cleanse myself of the memory. Dreams restored the dead, but never fully. One minute they are gone, the next they are back. Sleep was nothing more than a Groundhog's Day for the living. A nightly boomerang. In the morning, when grief returned—and it always did—it slammed like the wind.

At the tip of the peninsula I turned and followed the path to the beach, passed hammocks of pine scrub set against the white beaches and restless water. A flock of gulls screeched their petty battles, picking over the beach's debris: fish bones, seaweed, stranded conchs, and skittish fiddler crabs. The stench of low tide. A few porpoises breached out in the deeper water, chasing a school of mackerel.

I passed the Spanish ruins, so old they seemed like ancient boulders hidden in the landscape. The upper deck sat facing South with a view of the sunrise and sunset and any passing boat. The top level had a view of the gulf, the endless glare of sunlight bouncing off the surf. The pain it caused behind my eyes made me look away.

One time, Dad took me down below the upper deck to the rooms that had been dug out of the ground. Damp rooms filled with shadows. Chains bolted to walls. Local folk claimed these rooms were dungeons to hold pirates or slaves. They said those rooms were haunted by the ghosts of slaves and prisoners. Dad laughed at those stories and said that was rubbish. Ghosts don't exist. They were just empty storerooms where they kept their provisions.

When I got to the north end of the park, the beach was desolate. White sand stretched out for miles with no one else in sight. Pelicans flew in formation overhead, then dropped low to let their wings skim the water. A school of fish and a stingray swam past. The air was still, and the water flat and calm, a place so barren it might've been the surface of the moon.

As I waded out to a sandbar a hundred yards off shore, the water got deep. It came up to my knees, then got deeper still. The current was swift as I swam across.

On the sandbar, dozens of sand dollars and starfish had been stranded by low tide. They lay dead and bleaching in the sun. I skipped them like river rocks across the surface.

The sun beat down on my head. I dove underwater. Sunlight filtered prisms of yellow and green columns. Pieces of seaweed floated into view. As the specks came closer, they began to take shape. Seahorses. Just like the one Dad and I had found last year washed up on the beach. He had spotted it first, partially sticking out of a pile of seaweed. Dead and dried, a brown-ridged spine in the shape of an S. That day, we had counted ourselves lucky. We had tied a red ribbon around its neck, and hung it on the door of our small shack.

But the ones floating in the water before me were alive.

Another one floated into view and then another, each one no bigger than my thumb. Then there were dozens of them floating all around me, an entire school. If Dad had been there, he would have said it was pure luck. That I was a lucky girl.

They drifted into the current toward the end of the sandbar where the water turned cold. I followed them out there, but they stayed just beyond my reach.

The current was strong and the water was colder than a spring. I shivered. I gasped for air and water splashed into my mouth. The sandbar and the beach were out of sight but I could see tall pine trees in the distance. Green against a pale sky. I caught a breath, and dove toward land, but I got nowhere. I surfaced and tried to dog-paddle. The sun was high overhead but it did not warm me. My legs were chilled, the muscles stiffening. I fought to keep my eyes open. I couldn't stop shaking. My brain went dark. The tide pushed me farther out. Dad always said to not fight the current, to let it take you. It took me toward the mouth of the bay. I drifted, shivering and tilting in and out of this world. The pines were gone from view.

A dark shape appeared below me. Then another. They came close, disappeared and reappeared, rising and sinking in turns. The water darkened as the shapes congregated and offered an indifferent welcoming.

At the entrance to the bay the bridge stretched over the water, linking the peninsula back to the mainland. The water out there, deep as night. I had already forgotten my last breath.

The current took me beneath the bridge, but I could see from high above the water. The shore there was thick with wiregrass. Swampland. Greens and blues swirled below me as I lifted into the air. The world was no longer a tangible thing. Its smells and textures no longer mine. All of it a memory, no more real than the day my father and I found that dried-up seahorse on the beach. No more real than his hand slipping from my own.

Dad claimed there were no ghosts, only empty rooms full of rusted chains and broken doors. But he was wrong. In these deep waters, the dead are everywhere.

Racine

The minutes gathered at her feet, pooling there like water seeping through a crack below a door. With each minute that passed the tide grew higher and soon every chance to make up those lost moments would be gone, swept away like toys in a flood. Hours that Racine should have spent with her son were spent instead on the bus ride across town. It took one transfer and an hour to get to her job. Time. It was the one thing she could never afford and the only thing that might have made the difference. She hadn't tucked him in bed one night this whole year, hadn't made it to a parent teacher meeting, either. In fact, her only parental accomplishment lately was to fix him peanut butter and jelly sandwiches and leave them on the counter each morning before she left for work.

Now he sat quietly on the bench next to her sucking on the cherry lollypop that the officer had given to him after the interview. Sugar always quieted him down for the first few minutes until it got in his bloodstream, then he would turn wild. He was like any other child that way. His legs swung back and forth beneath the hardwood bench. For the moment he was content, almost oblivious. His hand, small and sticky, rested on her forearm.

Greed, she blamed it on her own greed. She spent two and a half hours a day and four dollars and fifty cents on the city bus, so taking a second job while she was already downtown had made sense, at the time. She never bargained that curiosity born out of boredom would lead him down the hallway to his uncle's room. Never figured he would find that pistol in the dresser drawer, much less take it to school and show it off. She didn't even own a gun, happy to let her brother handle the things, but in this Georgia county, the law read each and every household would own a firearm. She raked her mind. How had it come to this so soon? He was only eight years old.

She knew these would be the last minutes they would have together as clearly as she knew her own name. The wasted hours tore at her. Regrets. They'd been gathering their darkness in her soul since the day he was born.

She should have taken him right then and walked out of the building, sought the dream she'd imagined every day during the ride on that cold bus. It was always cold on the bus. In the mornings her feet felt like ice cubes. She wrapped her coat up snug around her neck and let the lull of wheels rolling against pavement drive her into the dream. It started out the same every time. When her next paycheck came, she would cash it and buy two one-way tickets to Florida. They'd go to Orlando a place so warm they could live in a city park until she found a job and a room to rent. She could transform their lives in two, maybe three months.

Or maybe she would spend the whole chunk on the lottery. She'd play the Fantasy Five where the odds of winning were better. Of course, the payout was smaller but it wouldn't take much to set them on the high road. A few thousand dollars. The amount didn't matter. In the dream, the money would make her calm and wise. Smart decisions would come naturally to her.

Half of it would go directly into a savings account. She would leave a hundred with her brother for taking them in last year after her boyfriend split town and left her with three months' back rent. With the other half she'd buy a small sedan, nothing fancy, used, but with power locks and heat that blew good. Then she'd invest in a wardrobe, something that would help her get a better job. A black suit with mix and match tops to stretch it out through the work week. It wouldn't be a splurge, only an investment in their future.

Clicking heels on the marbled hallway snapped her out of the dream. She didn't look up. She stared at the boy's hand resting on her arm trying to burn it into her memory.

A woman crouched down before them and introduced herself to the boy in a sweet cajoling voice. "Would you come with me?" she asked.

"Mama?" His hand moved off her arm as he slid off the bench.

She looked at him. The thick lenses of his glasses magnified his eyes. Those glasses had always unnerved her. She'd hoped they would give him an intelligent look, make him seem more dignified. Instead she was reminded of a shark they'd seen at the aquarium downtown last year.

"Go on now," she said. "I'll see you soon." She was glad he was leaving before the sugar got him stirred up.

The woman took the boy by the hand and led him away. Her steps echoed against the walls of the corridor. It was better this way. Let him cry his eyes out rather than throw a tantrum here in front of all these people. The world was her judge and jury now and every move she made from here on out would be scrutinized and documented.

Racine's hands lay in her lap, her fingers curled tightly around each other. She loosened her grip and lay her hand palm down on the place where he'd been, collecting the warmth left behind by his small body. Why hadn't she led him away from this place, stood up two minutes sooner and walked out? The Greyhound station was one block south of City Hall. They could have gotten out of town, out of state. But she hadn't thought of it in time and she only had eight dollars in her purse anyway. It was like so many other moments in the course his young life when she'd been unprepared and two steps behind.

She left the building two hours later, after it had all been explained. Her son was in the custody of the state and in route to a juvenile facility where he would be evaluated and housed. She was free to go with the knowledge that charges might be levied against her pending further investigation.

A police woman was kind enough to show her a way out of the building where reporters and cameras could not pound her with questions and accusations.

Her son was the youngest person in the history of the county to be charged with attempted murder. A foolish spat turned into a deed no one could undo; a nine-year-old girl lay half dead in the hospital's emergency room. Numb with shock, Racine walked the three miles home, carrying her coat over her arm, to save the bus fare.

The apartment was empty. She watched the local news on their old portable television. Her brother had been arrested within an hour of the shooting. They found him easily, traced the gun registered in his name, found the auto parts store where he worked and picked him up without a struggle. She was glad he hadn't been shot. Her brother was led from the store in handcuffs, hiding his face in the red hoodie she'd given him last Christmas. The handcuffs made him look dangerous though he'd never had a run-in with the police. Local television stations covered the story with teams of cameras and satellite trucks. There was also a helicopter view of her son's school surrounded by a dozen police cars and three ambulances. A reporter stood beside the entrance to the county hospital speaking into a microphone, his face appropriately grim, his eyes fired up by gory details. She turned the sound off.

She spent the night on the sofa staring at the ceiling. Rest was a luxury she did not deserve. In the small hours after midnight, she found a few hours of amnesiac sleep. At four a.m. a voice shattered the silence: "The girl is dead."

She sat up, baffled, and searched the apartment. No one was there.

The constant news crawl on CNN confirmed it.

She waited for the police to come. Nothing. No one called, no one came.

Two days passed. On Monday morning she went to the juvenile detention center and asked to see her son. He was being assessed by psychiatrists. She waited five hours to see him through a wired glass window. He cried when he saw her, over the phone line she told him to be brave. When he got hysterical two men took him away. They left her alone in the small visiting room; she broke down for the first time. An hour later she realized they weren't going to bring him back and she left.

A co-worker dropped her paycheck off at the apartment. Inside the envelope was a note telling her she was fired. The next day she cashed it and went back to see her son. He became hysterical again and tried to break through the glass window. He screamed for her to take him home. They carried him away. A man came in saying he was the defense attorney appointed by the state. He hadn't shaved in days and his cheap blue suit was stained and wrinkled, but that and the dark circles beneath his eyes made her trust him. He advised her not to come back for a few days so the boy could adjust to his new environment. She went home.

The bills were due, but this month they would wait. She had seven hundred and three dollars. A cousin had agreed to put up bail for her brother and her son would be better off not seeing her. She put half the money in an envelope, left it on the kitchen table and packed her suitcase. Fifteen minutes later, without a glance around the room, she walked out the door. She needed to feel wheels rolling down the highway, needed to travel, and needed someplace different, a place where the future was not already destroyed.

At the bus station she studied the names of towns to the south, finally choosing one that would take twenty-seven hours to reach. A lifetime. She used her coat as a pillow leaning the chair back as far as it would go. The rhythm of the wheels rocked her, wrapped her in a soothing reality. They stopped in sleepy towns and at the intersections of small highways to let other passengers on and off. She slept, and, now and then, in her sleep, her memory was wiped clean.

They traveled through the night. It didn't last forever. The next morning, her fare ran out. She tried not to wake up, but the driver came to her seat. He touched her foot lightly with his own.

"Excuse me, miss. This is the end of the road for you."

She opened her eyes and peered through the window of the bus. They were parked at the bus station in Clearwater Beach just across the street from the Gulf of Mexico. Hotels windows glared in the sunlight and she held a hand over her eyes, straining to see across the road.

She carried her suitcase across the street and set it down next to a bench. Someone had left a pair of sunglasses lying in the grass, she put them on. They helped some. At least she could see the place without squinting.

Before her lay a body of water larger than the mighty Mississippi, the only frame of reference she had for such a thing. The line where sky and water met stretched from one end of the horizon to the other. So, this was Florida, land of big water and broad skies.

She planned to live on the street until her money ran out. After that she didn't know and didn't care enough to sort through it. She stared at the waves breaking against the sand and let freedom ooze into her bones. She wasn't hungry, wasn't restless. Sitting by the gulf she was unwilling to think about the coming day. She sifted sand through her fingers. The world was larger than she'd ever known it to be and that knowledge expanded inside her lungs. The air was warm and breathing was all she needed to do.

The day melted into a sunset so beautiful it made her think of the gates to heaven. Shades of pink and yellow she'd only ever seen in candy flared across the sky. She watched the dusk dim to a purple night. Far away from home and unprotected, she expected to die in her sleep and she welcomed the thought.

In the dark, the full moon rose over the water. Its light so bright that she woke up thinking it was morning. A silver vision of light and water, it had to be a dream. But waking brought back the memory of the son she had left behind. Still, there was no hunger stirring inside. There was no one on the beach but herself. Leaving her suitcase and shoes behind she walked down the beach. The breeze danced across her skin.

Something wasn't right. She had no business feeling such comfort while her only child sat in confinement. She pushed the thought away.

The Milky Way streamed its silver dust in the darkness overhead. She stood in ankle deep water and wondered what it felt like to drown. She'd heard it was painless. The warm night air, the water at her feet. This moment of relief felt like betrayal.

Ghost crabs scrambled in the foam at the water's edge. Their lives were guided by the elements. A white heron glided out of the black night skimming the water with its wing tips. It landed a few yards away and scooped something into its mouth, stretched out its long neck to swallow. She looked closer.

A line of small creatures crawled out from the sand and headed toward the water. The heron scooped another into its beak. She knelt in the sand. Turtles, just now hatching. They were tiny things. They were digging their way out of a nest. With her eyes, she traced the procession back to a spot staked and taped off with yellow caution tape. A nest. They were hatching and digging their way out of a nest, emerging as if by magic, and crawling into the world of air and moonlight.

Wasn't there a mother somewhere? She guessed not. They had been left to fend for themselves, to become a feast for the heron. It craned its neck to see around her. She waved her hands and it jumped backwards. They faced each other, neither willing to give way. Slowly the heron picked its way around her and into the water, stepping over the waves with its thin legs. Several babies had reached the water and the heron lunged. It grabbed another one and swallowed quickly. The others made it to the water where a wave swept them to sea. She flailed at the heron again; it flew a circle around her and landed on the opposite side of the turtles.

Racine planted her feet. "Go on now!" she yelled, waving her hands. The heron flailed backwards, wings beating against the black night. It stepped further away and folded its wings to wait.

There might have been a hundred turtles that climbed out of the sand that night, she couldn't count them all. Each one found its way to the Gulf by crawling past her wet and sandy feet. Those who started out the wrong way she picked up and placed nearer the water. The folded heron watched. When it seemed that the last turtle had left the nest, Racine sat and sifted through the sand with her fingers. The heron closed its eyes and slept.

She found a place in the sand dune where the breeze was stilled and watched the moon travel to the other end of the sky.

The next morning, she stuffed her suitcase under the bench, hoping it would be there when she got back and not caring if it wasn't. She went for a walk through the town and found a small park with a pond.

Across the pond, through the trees and shadows she saw a parking lot filled with chairs and people. They sat quietly, facing a building. It was a Tuesday morning in a month without any holidays. She couldn't imagine why people would sit in a parking lot in the sun on a day in the middle of the week.

She walked around the edge of the pond, stirring up a flock of ducks. At an intersection she checked the traffic light before stepping into the street. Halfway across she froze. A yellow cab swerved to miss her, and seconds ticked by before time and sound caught up with her. A police officer took her by the elbow and guided her out of the street.

It wasn't the five-story image of a woman's head and upper torso that caught her. It wasn't the colors blending into a rainbow to form a silhouette. It wasn't the question of how such a thing could happen. It was the slight tilt of the woman's head, the expression of forgiveness, that took her breath away.

It was a simple office building, fifty feet high and made of steel and glass. But the windows of the building had somehow been burnished or stained in a specter of earthly colors. Very clearly, in the center of the vision, was Mary. Racine was overwhelmed by an excruciating flood of forgiveness. And then she felt the full weight of her son in her arms.

Something solid inside her chest knocked against her spine. Maybe it was her heart giving out. She stumbled to an abandoned lawn chair. As she reached the chair, something in her broke free; she fell to her knees and let herself exist in a state of yearning. Suddenly, the madness of her own life seemed small.

She scanned the area for a clue as to what to do. People milled around the building; there seemed to be no one in charge, no one to pay. Some took photographs; others sat in prayer, most simply stood and stared. One scraggly-looking man hawked rosaries and homemade postcards of the image.

She would remember the day forever and sometimes wonder if it had been real. She kept a postcard with her to remind her that it was. It was that moment she would look back on, the moment when all her questions became bearable.

On her third day in Florida, she boarded the bus and took it back to the town where her son would spend his incarceration. There might come a time when seeing his mother did not tear the boy apart, but she would have years to prepare for that day.

Freedom's Just Another Word

EXCERPT FROM *The Girl From Blind River*

That morning, after an eternity of winter gloom, the sun finally came out, busting through the window and slanting across Toby's eyes. He pulled on his boots and jacket, stuck the box with the necklace in it deep in the front pocket of his jeans, and left for school. He was already late for first period but it was just study hall and who cared anyway? It was his mom's first birthday since she'd come back to town and he had a present for her. If he walked fast, he could get to the diner in twenty minutes. She worked the breakfast shift every morning, and unless she'd taken it off for her birthday, she'd pour him a cup of coffee like he was one of her regulars and he'd drink it while she shuffled plates of scrambled eggs and toast to her customers. He'd wait for things to get quiet, even if that meant skipping all his morning classes, and surprise her with the necklace. The scene played out in his head—her surprise, the happy tears in her eyes. He passed on his usual breakfast of two Snickers and a Monster from the 7-Eleven and cut straight through the woods to Main Street. The storefronts on Main—the hardware store, the Army recruitment center, the pawnshop, the insurance broker, the bank—were still closed, but the diner was open.

The bells on the diner's front door jangled when he stepped inside. His mom looked up from pouring coffee and, seeing her face, Toby realized he'd forgotten to buy a birthday card. A sergeant from the recruiting center came in right behind him and it was him that Phoebe attended to first by motioning to an open table by the window and handing him a menu. Customers always came first. He knew that. Besides, his favorite stool at the end of the counter by the kitchen door was vacant. Even before he sat down, she turned over a cup and filled it for him, said, "Morning," then went to take the sergeant's order. Her eyes and nose were red and puffy, and he wondered if she'd been sad to wake up alone, her first birthday after eight behind bars, and was glad he'd planned it this way. Women were healed in mysterious ways by presents of jewelry from the men in their lives. Despite having never done it himself, he'd seen this fact proven a thousand times on television. He'd never had the chance to create that kind of smile on a woman's face before today.

But she was here now, and he was here, and he'd planned the whole thing himself. He set the black box on the counter, leaned forward on his elbows, and kept it hidden under his hand. At the right moment he'd reveal the box and watch the surprise spread across her face. While she took a to-go order over the phone, he tore open three packages of sugar and filled his coffee with cream. She stuck the order through the cook's window and the cook snagged it, and then his mom came back to him.

She leaned over the counter. "I got here late and I can't talk much this morning." Her voice was rushed and low. She set a pamphlet next to his coffee. "This is for you. The recruitment officer comes in here every morning. He said you can apply before your eighteenth birthday if you have a parent sign." She wasn't her usual self, but that's what he'd come here to fix. He pushed the box toward her—she hadn't noticed it yet—and said, "Happy birthday."

She stared flatly at the box and Toby realized she didn't understand. She'd gone without for too many years.

"It's for your birthday. Open it." He flinched when she stepped away and straightened her back.

"What is that?" She wiped her hands on her apron and glanced sideways down the counter.

He slid the box toward her. She didn't take it, so he opened it for her. "Happy birthday," he said again, more as an explanation than anything.

She frowned. "How did you afford that?" She was whispering, but people were noticing now.

The necklace was too simple. He should've known she'd want something nicer, bigger, better. A tiny silver cross on a thin chain. How could he be so stupid?

"Let me put it on you," Toby said, but Phoebe snagged the box and shoved it in her apron pocket. "I'll put it on later. Let me get you something to eat."

His face reflected hers now and his mood went tumbling toward that empty feeling he couldn't name but hated anyway. He saw a string hanging around her neck. A string, when she could have worn this necklace. "I'm not really hungry," he said, knowing that empty feeling would be with him the rest of the day. The cook slammed his bell and called, "Order up." Phoebe went to the pass-through and grabbed the steaming plates.

Toby's eyes felt hot as he sat there at the counter, trying to recover. The pamphlet showed a picture of a soldier driving a tank across the desert. He knew what happened to those guys. They came home as heroes, smiling in their uniforms and prosthetics like they were still whole men, but what did the uniform matter when they'd been blown up by cowards who dressed like women and hid behind children? And how could she want him to leave, especially after she'd just come back?

"Don't you need to get to school?" She returned to refill his coffee cup, but it was still full.

"You don't like it."

She reached over and touched the back of his hand. "I like it, honey. I just don't want to get it dirty while I work. I'll put it on later, okay? After my shift."

"John, over by the window, gave me this. He said for you to come talk to him at the recruitment center." She unfolded the pamphlet and spread it on the counter. Inside there were more pictures of soldiers, men and women, a guy walking through a crowd of dancing kids.

"Have you thought about what you'll do after graduation?" she asked.

"I'm working with my uncle."

"What? That's not a career. You should join the Army and learn a real trade."

"And get blown up."

She glanced toward the recruitment officer. "Shhh, Toby. You could have a life, get out of Blind River for a few years, come back, and build your own family."

"I don't want a family." How could she say this to him? She wanted him to leave? All those years spent waiting for her to come home. All those years wondering what she could possibly have done that they'd taken her from him, her child, and locked her away. He'd cried so hard that first year, believing that she'd be home soon, not understanding, not accepting, just waiting and waiting for her to come back before finally getting it, getting that she wasn't ever coming home. And when he grew tired of crying, he'd started hitting things, then people. Hitting Jamie, hitting kids at school, hitting anything he wanted whether it meant a broken knuckle or not. Hitting was better than crying. He knew that much. But he wouldn't hit his mother even though right now it seemed like she deserved it. Instead, he picked up the brochure, ripped it in half, and walked out the door.

He walked down Main cussing and rubbing the corners of his eyes, his nose that had started to drip. Snow crunched beneath his boots. He cut across the soccer field with its frozen brown grass, bent and dead from the winter. She'd been gone most of his life and he'd been fine without her. Bitch. Most mothers took care of their kids; most mothers didn't steal shit and go to prison. He pushed open the school door and instantly wondered why he'd come. But he knew why. Inside these walls were people and what he needed right now was someone to hit.

He stopped and turned to leave, but the second-period bell sounded and the halls filled with kids, so he put his head down and pulled his collar up around his chin and tried to cruise past the front office.

Ms. Hollins and Coach Palmer stepped out of their weekly staff meeting just as he, fists clenched in his pockets, rounded the corner.

"Hold up there, boy," Palmer said, and put his hand on Toby's shoulder. "School started an hour ago."

Toby flinched and pushed the man's hand away. "Keep your hands off, faggot."

"What? In my office now, Toby. You need to cool down." Ms. Hollins waved her hand in Toby's face.

"No!" Toby yelled. He didn't want to be here one minute longer. He hated this place, hated these people. He turned to back toward the doors, but Coach grabbed his arm. Toby wheeled on him, came around swinging his fist at no one, at anyone, at everyone, at nothing and everything, at the first thing stupid enough to stand still and let him connect.

Beyond the tiny, wire mesh-covered window, the small square of sky was the color of steel. Toby balled up the thin mattress from the built-in concrete shelf and stood on it. Who the fuck puts a window seven feet off the ground? Daylight was fading, but if he pulled himself high enough, he could almost make out the roof of a building he judged to be about a football field away. The mattress slid out from under him and when he landed, he smacked his elbow against the metal toilet. He held his arm and rocked back and forth, trying to breathe.

Being locked up wasn't as scary as he'd thought it would be, but all the same, he fucking hated it here. All this steel and concrete. It wasn't natural. Tiny mesh windows bolted closed, big guards pushing him around, everything locked up tight, no Xbox. Somewhere down the long corridor he could hear a TV blasting a Judge Judy marathon, her voice a parrot screech in his brain. There was nothing to hit but the walls, nothing to kick or break. His legs ached to run, and now his elbow throbbed. The biggest guard on the cell block walked past his door and glanced in. He carried the standard gear on his belt: a can of mace, a nightstick, and plastic restraints.

"Sir? Sir?" Toby had been in the center twenty-four hours and no one had spoken to him since they'd processed his fingerprints and locked him in this room.

The guard stopped and faced the cell door. "What?"

The sound of a human voice nearly brought him to tears. He stepped closer to the door and read the man's badge. "Brewster, huh? It's lonely in here, you know? You're the first one to talk to me."

"Must be the first time you said sir."

"What?"

"You want to address someone in here, you call them sir. Understand?"

"Yeah."

"Yes, sir," Brewster said and turned away.

"Wait!" Toby called. He refused to cry, but that only made his nose run. He swiped at it, hating the pleading tone in his voice and how it made him feel like a girl.

"Sir!" Toby yelled. "You got any Red Man?" But the man kept walking.

Toby took a piece of toilet paper and folded it until it was a small tight square, stuck it between his cheek and teeth like he'd done when he was little and starving. He sucked at it, slumped on the mattress, and tried to think why his uncle hadn't shown up yet. Or Jamie. She was nineteen now. Didn't that mean she could bail him out?

An hour later the man returned.

"Sir," Toby said. Brewster stopped and faced the boy's door again.

"What?"

"Why am I here? I threw one punch. What's the big deal?"

"You punched the high school coach."

"He got a bloody nose is all," Toby said, moving closer to the door.

Brewster stepped in front of the opening, his height blocking the light. "You broke his nose."

Toby feigned a right hook. "I can't help he's a pansy, can't take a hit."

Brewster's face was flat, his hands big as paddles, an eagle in military green tattooed on his forearm. Toby smelled the stink of a rotten tooth and backed away.

"Hey, nice tattoo, man. Army?"

"Marine Corps. Retired."

Despite the bad breath he liked Brewster and wanted to keep him talking. "I'm joining soon as I graduate."

"Huh. Don't know they take punks."

"They'll take me. One of 'em will. Army, Navy. Hey, man, I came in with some Red Man. Can I get it?"

"Don't know if you noticed, but this is a jail. Ain't no room service in here."

"I want my stuff!"

The cell was too small, the light too low. Someone turned up the volume on the Judge Judy marathon.

"Your stuff is at the front door. You get it on your way out."

Toby gripped the bars and shook them. Nothing moved, nothing even rattled.

Brewster didn't flinch. "Settle down. You're not going anywhere soon."

"Where's my uncle? I'm a juvenile!" He pushed away from the door. "You can't keep me here! I got rights! Where's my sister?" He was trembling with rage.

"See now, that's where you're wrong. You got nothing, boy. Assault with intent to harm? At your age, that don't get you sent to juvie. This here's downtown jail."

Toby picked up the mattress and threw it, kicked it, kicked it again, fell on it and tried to rip it in half.

"You best calm down, boy," Brewster said.

"Don't tell me to calm down!" Toby screamed. From somewhere deep in his belly a howl made its way through to his lungs and out his mouth. He beat his head with his fists.

The door clanged on its hinges and three officers rushed in. Brewster caught Toby's arm and bent it behind his back. Another man guarded the door. The third man picked up the mattress, folded it like a sheet, and walked out the door.

"You're going to have to earn that back," Brewster said.

Toby jerked to get loose but Brewster pulled his arm tighter. Pain shot through his shoulder, and Toby dropped to the floor.

Brewster let go of his arm and pushed him to the far wall. "Let me know if you can't get that back in its joint," he said, and slammed the steel door shut.

Toby yanked his boot off and bashed the heel against the window latch. The latch broke off but the window frame was frozen with rust and it wouldn't budge. His lip throbbed, his head banged, his vision was blurred. Beating the shit out of him and locking him in the back room of the trailer only proved how fucked up his uncle Loyal was. No way Toby would stay here and wait for the bastard to come back for round two. He'd take this trailer apart before he'd stay locked up in here one more day. He broke the window and knocked out the glass fragments until it was wide enough to climb through, then went around the outside of the trailer to the front door which, go figure, his uncle had left unlocked. Inside the bathroom he checked his lip in the mirror, soaked a towel, and wiped the dried blood, which only opened the cut and set it bleeding again. He jumped at the sound of a car's engine, relaxed when he realized it was just a neighbor.

At first, he'd been relieved when Loyal had shown up at the jail to post bail, couldn't wait to get away from that guard. But as soon as they got in the truck, he realized he'd been safer in that cell. Bail was a thousand bucks and Loyal had ranted on the ride home about how much money Toby had been costing him lately. Toby had promised to make it up if Loyal would give him a job, but Loyal had shouted no and drained his flask. As soon as they got inside the trailer Loyal had taken off his belt. He was pretty sure the welt over his eye had come from the buckle, hated how he'd cried out when metal connected with bone. When Loyal got tired he'd stopped, grabbed his coat, and locked him up in the back room. No doubt he was at some bar right now getting tanked on whiskey and beer chasers and when he got home there'd be nothing holding him back. Toby splashed water on his face, the lump below his eye still swelling.

The beating wouldn't have been so bad if Jamie had been home. Loyal always pulled his punches in front of her. Goddamn her. She was probably with her pervert boyfriend. Goddamn all of them. He held a towel to his lip and went to Loyal's room to rummage through the box under his bed where he kept his stash of nudie postcards from his buddy in Key West. There was almost always money in that box, and today he found a wallet with a few bills and credit cards belonging to some schmuck named Theodore James Bangor, and the extra keys to the old truck. He stuffed the wallet in his pocket and grabbed his jacket and a box of Pop-Tarts, paused at the door and looked around for something more, but there wasn't anything more and he walked out the door.

He took the long walk that wound through the back valley and headed toward town. It had once been a cornfield, but land speculators, predicting a boom, had bought up all this acreage years ago. The boom fizzled the year after the fertilizer plant exploded and left a cloud of toxic smoke hanging over the town for a month. Now it was an empty field of brown weeds, not even fit for grazing. Standing water sloshed under his boots. He looked at the land his grandfather, Nate Elders, used to own. Twenty acres. Some of it turned into a trailer park, some of it set aside as a dump. If the old man hadn't sold out, they'd still be farmers. Maybe they'd still have cows, maybe a tractor. Maybe a good life. Toby went up the rise on the other side of the valley and took the road to town. He needed to find Jamie. She'd know what to do, maybe help him find somewhere to hide for a few days until Loyal cooled off. Maybe they'd go away together on the bus like they'd always wanted. They were older now and no one would care if they bolted. Kids did that all the time. No one would even look for them. When he got to town, he took the alley that ran parallel to Main. He thought about stopping by the diner, but his mother was so weird now. He'd paid a hundred dollars for that stupid necklace and she'd hated it. Fucking waste of time. He saw the Ford sitting on Main where his sister had left it.

He'd rather drive head on into a pylon or off a bridge than endure another minute of this bullshit town. The engine started the third time he cranked it and he floored it down Main Street. When he turned East on the county road the town disappeared in his rearview mirror. *Good riddance Blind River.*

He got a hundred miles away before he ran out of gas and had to flag down a passing truck. The window lowered as it pulled to the shoulder, and a skinny old man with a neck too stiff to turn leaned his head out.

"Out of gas," Toby said.

The old man said, "It happens. One of them cans in the back might have something in it." He pointed a crooked finger up the road. "There's a station, ten miles up this road. Should be enough to get you there."

The back of the old man's truck was full of garbage: bags of aluminum cans, a broken weed eater, unrecognizable spare parts thick with grease, three gas cans. Toby found a small one that was half full. He grabbed it and the truck pulled back onto the road.

"Wait!" he yelled, but the old man just waved out the back window, his back wheels spinning gravel at Toby's feet.

The gas station was closer to twenty miles away. Toby coasted in on fumes and radio static. The cashier was a wiry girl with sunken cheeks and a blue tattoo crawling down her arm that read Reveal Your Soul. He smiled at her to test the possibilities. She glared back, and he wondered what kind of girl would have a tattoo like that and not smile at a guy.

"Turn the pump on?"

"Sign says prepay."

The money he'd taken from under Loyal's bed amounted to twenty-eight dollars. "Give me twenty," he said, and got three Snickers bars and a six-pack of Cherry Cokes with the rest.

She flipped a switch for the pump and turned back to a small TV—that dyke talk show host who always wore sneakers and cut her hair like a boy.

"What's it mean?"

"What?"

"Your tattoo. What's it mean?"

"It's English. You know English?"

"Yeah."

"Then figure it out." She rolled her eyes and turned up the volume with the remote. He lost interest because girls like that were never fun. He headed to the truck and started the pump, then found the bathroom on the side of the building. The toilet was brown and furry so he pissed in the corner, threw water on his face, and dried off with five yards of paper towels. All his life he'd loved pulling paper towels out of those machines and the righteous feeling that came from wasting the stuff.

As he stepped outside a guy rounded the corner from the back of the station. He was narrow at the waist with a forward lean that made him look slinky and dark eyes that he kept aimed at the ground except for a single glance when Toby let him pass on the concrete walkway. His long black hair trailed behind him smelling like fresh water. Before he could block the thought, Toby realized the boy was the prettiest thing he'd ever seen up close and a crazy longing opened up inside his belly. He started to speak but tripped off the walkway and landed on his stomach in the dirt. The boy just smiled and went inside the bathroom. He left the door cracked and Toby sat in the dirt not knowing what to do. His dick pulsed against his leg; a reaction so wack he wanted to strangle the thing. The crazy sensation in his belly made him want to run hard and fast, but the boy's smile—he wanted to see that again. He stood up and slapped the dirt off his pants.

He was wondering what to do when a semi pulled off the highway and stopped at the farthest edge of the parking lot. A big bearded man in a camo ball cap tugged low over his brow left the truck's engine running and hurried to the bathroom. He shut the door solidly behind him without even noticing Toby standing there, his dick going soft. That boy's thin hips, that man's burly torso. His mind tumbled through a dozen scenarios. He wanted to go in there but his feet wouldn't budge. The crazy in his groin settled into a not-unpleasant sensation that he could live with and he turned away.

By the time Toby made it back to the pump, it had clicked off. Seventy-eight dollars and fifty-seven cents. The cashier was watching him out the window. He raised his hands as if to say thanks.

She pushed the window open and shouted, "You got to pay for that."

"It was supposed to shut off at twenty!"

"No, you were supposed to shut it off at twenty. The cops will explain how it all works if you want." The phone was in her hand.

She slid behind the register when he followed her inside.

Toby tossed what money he had on the counter. "It should've cut off."

"Not my problem you don't know how to use a pump."

He might've used the bogus credit card but now he was pissed-off. Heat pulsed in his cheeks and scalp. The part about blushing he hated the most was when it brought tears to his eyes, some kind of bad wiring in his head he hadn't yet outgrown so he decided to let her eat the difference. Outside the big plate window, the pretty boy was walking toward the highway and Toby watched to see which direction he would turn. The semi started rolling out of the parking lot. Those two hadn't been inside that bathroom for more than five minutes.

The boy got to the highway and Toby was thinking through the possibilities of spending the afternoon with him when a southbound car stopped and the boy got in. It was a relief in a lot of ways.

Fifteen miles east on I-15, Toby had eaten one of the Snickers and finished two Cherry Cokes, but he couldn't get that boy's smile or that girl's stupid tattoo off his mind. What the hell did it mean? An eighteen-wheeler passed and blew the Ford slightly toward the shoulder. He tried the radio, but this far out in the country, there was nothing but static.

For the first time in his life he was on his own. He loved the rolling hills, the horizon always out of reach. Another half-dozen semis passed him going west and he watched them flanking each other in his rearview mirror. Big trucks like that could take a body clear across the country a hundred times a year. He finally found a station playing Joplin, popped another Cherry Coke, and made up his own lyrics.

"Freedom's just an open road and nothing left to do." He slapped the steering wheel, wondering where he could get his hands on a semi. Toby thought about the boy again and the hair on his arms stood up. He'd never known a boy could be pretty. He imagined the two of them riding down the highway, sharing a joint with the windows rolled down, their hair blowing free.

Toby was taking a piss in a field behind a small bale of hay when a cruiser pulled up and stopped behind the truck. The officer stayed in the car with his warning lights cutting at the bright sky. Toby tucked his head. Behind him was a barbed-wire fence and beyond that a bare field extending to the top of a hill. The cover of nightfall was hours away. Another cruiser pulled in front of the truck and backed up until the truck was trapped between them. He'd feel better if they'd just turned off the damn lights.

The second cop, a big round guy, got out. He couldn't believe that girl had called the cops over sixty bucks. The big round guy drew his gun and crept up to the window. Toby buttoned his pants and stuck the stolen wallet deep into the hay where it wouldn't be found for months, and by then, hopefully some damn cow would have chewed it up and turned it to shit.

They checked the inside of the cab. Maybe this was just routine. Cops find an empty truck; they check it out. Standard. No big deal. They'd probably let him go if he came out and explained he was just taking a piss. He'd apologize for the confusion; cops loved apologies. He practiced saying it in his head. *Sorry, Officer; sorry for the confusion.*

He stepped out from behind the bale. The cops were studying the hinge on the tailgate, picking at something stuck there. One of them got a camera out of his pocket.

Toby yelled, "Hello." The cop with the camera jumped behind the truck, but the fat one dropped into a crouch and aimed his gun at Toby.

"Get down, motherfucker! Get down on the ground."

The barrel of that gun seemed as big as a canon. Toby raised his hand but his knees caved on their own accord. The first cop fumbled with the safety latch on his holster. In a heartbeat, another 9mm was pointed at Toby's head. Another cruiser pulled up and another gun was drawn.

Toby fell forward, partly out of compliance and partly because of gravity, but mostly because the sky had begun to cartwheel. "I'm . . . I'm sorry for the confusion, officer," Toby mumbled as he hit the ground.

Low Tide

The girl woke at midnight to the sound of water and stepped into the dark
hallway outside her bedroom. Her mother stood at the kitchen sink in a
rumpled yellow house dress, pouring a glass of water over the shriveled
potted ivy on the windowsill. When the woman picked up her car keys, the
girl stepped into the moonlit kitchen.

"Where are you going, Mom?"

"For a drive."

"I'm coming with you." The girl expected her to say no, but her mother
walked out the front door.

They drove south through town on the old bay road past the smokehouse
where the smell of wood and mackerel hung in the air. They passed the
bowling alley where her father had tried to teach her the game but what she
learned was that a gutter ball would make him laugh.

He'd been buried a month now.

The drawbridge was up where the road curved west and the bridge
crossed the intercoastal. The lights on the guard arm blinked yellow against
the black sky. The girl and her mother waited as a boat passed below and
the drawbridge lowered. The night watchman raised the guard arm and
waved them through.

Beyond the flat one-story motels lay a stretch of deserted beach. A breeze from the gulf blew across the dunes and bent the sea oats toward land. Her mother got an old quilt from the trunk and gave it to the girl to wrap around her shoulders.

Despite the warm night air, the sand cooled the soles of their feet and chilled their skin. Low tide had left bits of shells, fish bones and seaweed, scattered like shrapnel along the shore. Seagulls slept in small clusters. A white heron flew down the beach. The sky was shot through with stars, evidence that the world still spun.

They walked a mile then spread the blanket and laid on it. Moonlight reflected on the waves, lit her mother's face. Her mother seemed to fall asleep and so the girl curled in a ball and closed her eyes too.

When she woke, her mother was sitting up cross-legged and staring at the horizon.

"We should go," she said.

They stood to leave, but a large object appeared at the water's edge. Awkward and lumbering in the lapping waves. Half-submerged and dark, the girl's first thought was of driftwood, but it moved with the purpose of an animal.

"In all my years," her mother said.

"What is it?"

"A sea turtle coming ashore to lay her eggs."

Small waves crashed over its back. It heaved forward, trailing bits of seaweed and foam. It stopped at a spot between two sand dunes and started digging a hole.

Her mother whispered, "This is her beach. They say that a turtle lays her eggs in the same place she was born."

The sand was soft. It didn't take long to dig a hole a yard wide and a foot deep.

"She'll lay her eggs and leave." Her mother sat down to watch. "If the raccoons don't get them, a few will survive. But not many."

Perfectly round eggs dropped from beneath her tail and rolled into the nest.

"She doesn't stay?"

"No, she buries them and leaves."

"But who raises them?"

"They don't need raising. They hatch and crawl to the water."

"All alone?" the girl asked, but the woman wasn't listening.

The turtle, her eyes glazed with labor, never seemed to notice them. An hour later she'd laid more than sixty eggs. She kicked at the sand until they were covered then turned back toward the water.

The woman went to the turtle and placed the palm of her hand on her shell. At first the creature didn't seem to notice, but then she stopped and turned her head. She sniffed the air between them. The woman lifted her hand away. She followed the turtle into the water. The girl followed her mother.

The water came to the girl's knees as they walked. Her mother knelt and pushed herself alongside the turtle. It got deeper and the girl wondered if the woman meant to return at all. The mother and the turtle crawled silently, the waves breaking over their backs.

Further out the bottom gave way to underwater cliffs and currents. The turtle swam away, leaving her offspring to survive or not, to find the sea or not. The tide was at its still point. Soon, the water would begin to rise.

The girl stood chest-deep in the black water hoping to see the turtle one last time, losing sight of them both as they disappeared in the current.

Morning yellowed on the horizon. A breeze crossed the sky. She shivered and waded back to dry land. She shook the sand from the quilt, wrapped it around her shoulders, and sat down to wait.

Long Time Coming

Dory Hastings stirs as the first light of sun lifts the edges from a cool spring night. The curtains in the window shift slightly; a dream recedes. She rotates her left foot clockwise then back around the other way, rolls stiffly to her good side to sit up on the side of the bed and wrestles the cast on her left arm into its sling. The old ranch house is unfamiliar, though she was born here nearly twenty years prior. The smell of coffee wafts up from the downstairs kitchen and she figures her aunt is already working through the task of putting breakfast on the table. She'll have to stay here until she finds work or decides about school.

The hazy image of the dream reappears. Though his face is obscured she knows this is her father. He is walking toward her through a thick morning fog. If she closes her eyes maybe she can coax the next frame from its sleepy hiding place. He stops a few feet before her and she sees the horse sliding out of the fog, a black mare, graying along the length of its nose, led by a simple leather cord. Her father doesn't speak but his meaning is clear. She takes the lead from him, her fingers brushing his. The fog curls around his legs, his arms, his head, finally reclaiming him totally. Only the horse remains, waiting patiently, eyes brown and serene. It's the only dream she's ever had of him and she wants to hold on to it, put it inside a locket and wear it against her heart. But dreams are like a morning breeze that float around of their own accord

and there's nothing she can do to draw him out. Still, she is suffused with
pleasure.

She shuffles to the bathroom and turns on the tap, splashes water on her
face. The rehab therapists taught her how to get a t-shirt on over the cast. It's
difficult and time consuming but she gets it done and then yanks on a pair
of jeans and her old sneakers with the Velcro closures. Downstairs, Brenda
pours her a cup of coffee and wants to know if she slept well, if the bed was
comfortable. Her uncle appears behind the back screen-door, stomping his
boots to get the muck off, sees her and asks if she's ready.

She looks beyond him to where the old black mare is saddled and waiting,
and gives him a doubtful look.

"It's a place to start," he says.

To put it plain, Burdine and Clara married too young, a ranch boy and a
town girl, neither of them yet eighteen. They'd dated a few months in their
senior year, got drunk on prom night and made a baby that bound them
together. Love not being the deciding factor, their parents took them to
the courthouse. The wedding picture shows tall Burdine in a stiff white
shirt, black tie, and Stetson, holding the hand of curly headed, blue-eyed
Clara in an already too-snug yellow dress. Someone has reminded them to
smile at the camera. They named the baby Dory, after his mother, because
she was the one to deliver the girl during a thunderstorm at the Hastings'
ranch house.

Burdine opened a produce market in town and set up a simple, one
room apartment over the store. Clara tended the store while the baby slept
behind the cash register, tucked in a sturdy apple crate lined with a pink
chenille bedspread, a wedding gift from his mother. Burdine drove up and
down I-75 in a beat-up pick-up truck buying produce for the store.

In truck stops and at highway gas stations, dark-eyed, lanky Burdine
made friends easily. He was swiftly absorbed into a subculture of men,
married and not, who introduced him to a host of previously unknown
pleasures. After a year on the road, Burdine had come to terms with his

deeper predilections and they had nothing to do with women. Clara regretted that drunken prom night and the baby she was saddled with, but agreed to let Burdine go his own way in exchange for the store. There were plenty of produce truckers and they were happy to keep the store's bins filled. Before the baby was two years old, Burdine was on his way south to Key West. He visited the family ranch one last time. His parents, stubborn in the ways that ranchers are, made no attempt to hide their disappointment in their son. It wasn't long before Burdine was dead from a disease that, in his mother's words, "afflicted his kind."

A few years later, Clara met Hank and his son Wink at a bowling alley where she played in a singles league. Hank was still reeling, he and his son having recently fled an emotionally bankrupt home in Indiana to move to Biggs County. A Nazarene preacher, Hank confided that he'd been ousted from his church for divorcing his wife. A barrel-chested man, he'd been reduced to wrestling for money at the armory in town on Friday nights. He claimed there'd been no choice but divorce, and tearfully recounted his ex's persistent choice of liquor over their marriage. His tears were like a glacier melting at the onset of spring. Even though he was a divorced man, Clara viewed him as a widower who'd lost his wife to alcoholism, a disease that would have eventually killed her anyway. Clara, having watched "Love Story" far too many times, longed for an epic love of her own. Hank was an agonized soul she could rescue, and that boy needed a mother. She loved them both and that was that. A small Baptist wedding was planned.

Hank was unfamiliar with little girls. Considering the demise of the girl's father, he assumed the child would love him unconditionally. In a vain attempt to put things on the right track, he purchased a dress for Dory to wear at the wedding. He headed to Woolworth's and found the exact five-dollar dress he was looking for. Dory understood that appreciation for the present was in order, but found the dress repulsive. It was blue plaid with a built-in petticoat that jutted out below the waist like a hula hoop. Worse, it was edged with scratchy white lace at the neck and sleeves.

Despite mounting guilt, Dory could not bring herself to wear the dress. Making girls wear dresses was a curse she thought unfair. On the morning of the wedding she slipped into the only dress she'd ever found tolerable, a sleeveless brown shift.

Clara, tense as brides tend to be on their wedding day, came unglued and slapped Dory. "Put that blue dress on this minute! Don't even think about ruining this day for me!"

A stunned Dory understood her new status completely.

She wore the dress for an agonizing two hours, scratching at her arms and neck like a flea-bitten cat. Hank couldn't understand why the dress hadn't pleased the girl; he'd spent good money on it and had seen Shirley Temple wear a similar one in a movie. It shouldn't be this hard, he thought, to win the heart of a pitiful, fatherless girl.

After the wedding the two half-families were united as one and moved to a two-bedroom house. Hank built a thin partition in the corner of the den, making a bedroom for the pre-adolescent Wink, who immediately took to calling Clara "Mom." Dory considered the move contrived, since his own mother was still alive. Somehow, he had wormed his way into Clara's heart, a place her daughter considered barbed and wired shut.

Dory stuck the dress in the back of her closet. Over time, it became a sore reminder of the slap from Clara and the marriage. She never wore it again and was thankful when she finally outgrew it.

For a while, Clara and Hank discussed adoption. Dory eavesdropped, wondering if that meant she should call Hank "Dad." The subject was dropped when Hank and Clara realized it would mean the end of the monthly Social Security payments from Dory's deceased father.

Tension sizzled in the house when Hank, constantly running low on cash, admitted there were two more sons living with his ex-wife back in Indiana. The child support payments were hefty and the news set off a few fireworks before Clara adjusted. She kept the produce market running seven days a week. Hank found work on an as-needed basis at a car repair shop, his career as a Friday-night wrestler ruined by a twisted knee and a compressed disc in his spine.

A strained truce was negotiated between Hank and Dory. She never settled on what to call him, tried using Dad but thought that felt too intimate. She switched to Hank, but considering his adult status, that seemed presumptuous. Lost for a solution and confused by the ambiguity of their relationship, she avoided direct communication, a tactic that made conversation clumsy and friendship unlikely.

Wink earned his nickname as a toddler with a blocked tear duct. He was not an attractive boy but before the tear duct issue was resolved he'd learned that winking made him adorable to persons of the opposite sex. He never forgot the lesson and so the nickname stuck.

Wink bent his short but already muscular frame to every task Clara gave him. She found him useful and a mother-son bond developed. Money flowed to Wink through everyday chores that Dory's child-sized body could not yet manage. Mowing the lawn and heaving fifty-gallon garbage cans to the street was boy's work and paid a wage. Dory grew into the responsibilities of girlhood, laundry and house cleaning falling to her. It was understood these things were expected of her, that they were how she paid her way. The girl and boy, unrelated but under one roof, kept a wary eye on and a wide distance from each other.

Dory inherited a tall slender figure, brown eyes and a boyish jaw line from Burdine, and a pessimistic nature from her mother. She rarely mentioned her dad. Clara said he'd died of cancer but Dory wasn't sure. At thirteen, she showed a picture of Burdine to Wink. He laughed and blurted out, "Your dad was a fag!"

She studied the picture. Her father wore a pair of fringed blue jean shorts, cut far too short for a man, work boots, a gold necklace. His brown hair was longish and windblown. In a moment of confusion, Dory realized her father might have been a founding member of the Village People.

Later that night Dory took a pair of scissors to the photo. She cut across the bottom of the picture, removing the telling short shorts, until it appeared Burdine was wearing a regular pair of jeans. But she still saw the short shorts each time she looked at the picture, burned into her memory as they were. And she knew he had died in the late eighties, at the height of the AIDS epidemic.

Hank referred to Dory's dad as a Sodomite and insinuated that she'd inherited some latent genetic defect. The ex-preacher in Hank had a passion for pointing out temptations of the flesh, especially where women were concerned. "Remember," he said, "it was Eve who caused Adam to sin." He raised an eyebrow in a conspiratorial way that made Dory's skin crawl. Too young to recognize religious psychosis, she worried what he said was true, and wondered if she had repressed sordid inclinations lurking in her psyche.

In Dory's sophomore year, her high school hired a young, female coach for the girls' volleyball and basketball teams. Fresh out of college with startling blue eyes and spiky blond hair, every kid was fascinated by the sexy addition to the otherwise uninteresting faculty. Dory's teenage dreams, cloudy and unspecific but arousing to an alarming degree, revolved around the new coach. She spent the year avoiding her and failed Phys Ed. The following year, she was relieved to develop a crush on a greasy, long-haired boy with black fingernails, who never spoke to anyone and never once looked her way. His face might have been attractive, were it not fixed in a glare of perpetual annoyance. She mooned over him for hours, dreaming up stories about how he'd come to be so haunted. After several months of being ignored, and having run out of creative story lines, her interest waned.

Wink forged a path that worried Hank and Clara. He married a girl he worked with at the Winn Dixie and a suspicious six months later he was a father. Hank and Clara agreed there'd be no dating or boyfriends for Dory, not until after graduation. She simply shrugged at the edict and kept to herself that year—no dates, no social clubs, just the occasional movie night out at the mall with the nerdy kids from church.

In the middle of her senior year, Ms. Dunworth, her high school counselor, presented her with three options: enroll at the community college in the next county, enter the management training program at Waffle House, or apply for a cashier position at the Walmart that was currently under construction. Of the three choices, only one held any degree of hope. Dory considered her second-rate grades and contempt of textbooks.

"Community College? I thought that was for smart kids." Dory peered at the file spread open on the counselor's desk.

Ms. Dunworth flipped through her file, buying time for a response. With a 2.0 average, Dory wasn't really college material. How can a kid fail physical education? But the supervisor of schools insisted that every graduating senior be encouraged to enroll in community college.

Ms. Dunworth tapped a pencil on her desk. "Well, there's a series of developmental classes. You know, for students who need to catch up."

"I don't know." Dory stared out the window. All she'd ever known was the drudgery of surviving school each week in order to sleep late on Saturday mornings. She'd never thought much about the future. She mused silently that she might take a cue from her mother, get knocked up and trap some boy into marriage, make another generation miserable.

"Think about it, Dory." Ms. Dunworth rose from her chair. She didn't have time to sit with a girl who stared out the window, caught in daydreams. In one week's time, she was expected to counsel sixty graduating seniors, offering each the same options, varied slightly for the few who demonstrated some promise.

Outside the office, Dory passed the line of waiting students and headed across campus to the library. Overhead, crazy streaks of yellow crashed against a purpling sky, thrilling Dory. She secretly delighted in the occasional hurricanes that roared up Florida's Gulf Coast, though none had scored a direct hit on Biggs County in more than a hundred years. She'd learned to be content with thunderstorms and considered the twisting, spewing gales inevitable payback for the tedious stretches of hot, windless days that sucked the moisture from the air, filling it with dust that settled deep in the lungs. But for the occasional, solitary oak, dripping with Spanish moss,

Biggs County seemed nothing more than fifty-thousand acres of withering brown graze land, mounds of prickly brushwood, stumpy fields of boulders and dried-up watering holes. Dory couldn't fathom why her forebears chose to homestead in a place that annihilated the imagination and often cursed them for it.

Holed up inside the library's computer lab, she spent the next week searching for some way to escape, anything that would get her out of Biggs County and free her from Hank and Clara. The walls of the lab were lined with helpful ideas; a poster of a boy with a strong jawline dressed in military blue suggested she see the world. She'd aim lower and settle for seeing another state. From the computer, she learned everything she needed to know about Army enlistment procedures and there, in the solitary nest of a library study cubicle, Dory made the biggest decision of her life.

She started the paperwork right away and trained every day after school at the junior high school track. After two months she could do twenty push-ups, fifty sit-ups and run an eight-minute mile. By graduation, the paperwork was in place. She opened a bank account and started a list of the things she'd need to take with her.

Dory hated fighting with her mother and usually avoided it by closing herself into her room. Clara had insisted Dory enroll at the community college, knowing Social Security would continue sending monthly checks, provided the girl stayed in school. But Dory was done with school and had ignored her mother's instructions. She kept this to herself for as long as possible, until boot camp was just two days away. She expected an eruption and steeled herself for a fight; as anticipated, the announcement sent Clara into a rage.

"What am I going to do without those checks? You know Hank still owes child support on his boys. You can't just pull the rug out from under us without any warning!" An hour filled with a litany of Dory's flaws—her selfishness and the probability that she'd never amount to anything—wore Dory to tears. But she stood her ground.

"I'll send my paycheck home. And you won't even have the expense of feeding me." Clara quieted as she calculated the truth of that statement; the solution calmed her immediately. Convinced that leaving was the only way to sanity, Dory would happily buy her way out of that house. She retreated to her room.

The following day, tight-lipped and sullen, she walked to a nearby liquor store and asked the owner for some empty boxes. In the privacy of her room, she packed away the remnants of her childhood. She laid low all day, determined not to draw attention to her plans again. Tomorrow she'd escape this life that her ill-conceived birth had created. The awful blue dress she put in the bottom of a plastic garbage bag to be dropped off at the Salvation Army. She pitied the little girl it would fall to.

The last item to go into the box was an old alarm clock CD player that her mother had given her for her twelfth birthday. Clara believed presents should be useful items and had been tired of waking the girl for school each morning. She bought the alarm clock unaware that it included a radio and CD player. Dory had thought it the finest birthday gift she'd ever received, the ability to wake to music every morning. Now, she wrapped it in newspaper, gently placed it near the top of the last box, and then folded the box flaps clockwise, jamming the last one into place. It was a satisfying sight, her life tucked neatly into five boxes.

It had taken three weeks to collect the gear she'd need and she'd hidden the stash beneath her bed. Shoe polish, black wool socks, a week's worth of underwear, foot powder and cream, moleskin, a cheap waterproof watch, the boxes of throat lozenges that she'd read were critical. A note pad, stamps, and a pre-paid calling card were stored in a zip lock bag. All this she stuffed into an old gray duffle bag that had been in her closet forever.

By tomorrow, the tempers of the night would have cooled slightly and she'd be able to leave with some peace of mind. Dory knew she'd made the best choice; the goose bumps that popped up on her arms every time she thought of leaving proved it.

The next morning, gusts from the outer bands of an approaching tropical storm slammed against the roof, lifting shingles with their intermittent blasts. The mini-blinds in Dory's small bedroom, yellowed with age and bent beyond repair, did little to conceal the outside view: a white plastic grocery bag blowing down the street like a tumbleweed, being chased by a witless brown mutt.

The bus to Missouri was scheduled to leave at one-thirty. Out in the Gulf, the storm gathered strength, a few hours away from crashing into the coast. The television weatherman worried aloud that the winds would swell to a threatening pitch by late that night, growing into a category one hurricane, an entity with a name all its own and twenty-four-hour coverage. By then she'd be on the Greyhound, shaking off the dust of Biggs County forever. She'd miss the first storm of the year but that was all she'd miss.

As she stacked boxes in her closet, a quiet thrill flittered through her mind. If her mother had walked into her room, would she have caught the slight smile, seen the tiny flicker in her daughter's eyes? Dory, practiced at concealing emotions, would never let that happen. In a place where the future mirrored the past like an endless, hazy highway, displays of anticipation would spark nothing but jealousy. She enjoyed the thrill for a moment and then turned her face blank, replacing the unreadable mask she'd perfected in adolescence.

"You ready yet?" Clara called down the hall toward Dory's room.

Dory took one last look around. Boxes packed, the room, once witness to the wide swinging rollercoaster of puberty, and the walls that had then been plastered with boy-band posters, now held no sign of its recent occupant. Her past was disappearing, as if a giant hand had reached down and swept it like dust under the bed. The only indication of who might have lived in the tiny bedroom was the bedspread—pink chenille—a wedding gift from a grandmother (her father's mother, she thought), her only remembrance of a woman she couldn't remember. Still, she regretted leaving it behind.

Anticipation pricked at her spine; the future was a breath away, a clean slate that she would paint with smart colors and bold strokes. The Army promised the opportunity to be all that she could be. She would prove Hank wrong: she would become a soldier and contribute to the security of their country. She was not more trouble than she was worth.

In the mirror she saw a reflection that pleased her, her haircut new enough that she still startled. The look, she decided, made her seem older, more sophisticated. Until last week, her hair had fallen black and straight to the middle of her back. She'd cut it off herself, packaged it, and sent it off to a group in California she'd read about online that specialized in making wigs for cancer patients. She'd grown two inches in the last year and, with her recent training, all her baby fat had fallen away. She looked more like her father every day.

So. The day was finally here. Wink's wife had thrown him out recently, and this old room would be his now. The boy her mother didn't birth, but whom she unashamedly doted over, was a dismal failure at marriage. "No surprise in that," Dory thought. Clara had cheered up considerably when she'd heard the news of his imminent return, the boredom of living alone with Hank avoided. Clara would mend Wink's broken heart with home-cooked meals, chocolate cake, and endless rounds of Gin Rummy. And Dory would be a thousand miles away.

"I'm ready," Dory shouted toward the kitchen. She swung the duffle bag over her shoulder, the weight of it knocking her into a wall. She straightened and squeezed through the doorway.

"I'm dropping you off early," Clara said. "Amanda is fitting me in between some other clients." She slammed the car door, started the engine.

"Alright, I'll wait at the bus station." Dory thought the sooner they said goodbye, the sooner that tight feeling in her stomach would disappear.

At the station, Clara pulled into a parking space, left the engine running and got out. She grabbed Dory in a hug. Dory's arms hung by her sides. She stared at her mother, not understanding.

"People hug when they say goodbye." Clara offered as an explanation.

Dory lugged her duffle bag to the counter and bought a one-way ticket to Missouri. There were two hours to kill so she found a bench where she could people watch. Lots of them hugged. When they said hello and when they said goodbye. She decided there were two types of families; ones that hugged and ones that didn't. Hers wasn't the hugging kind and she was okay with that.

Nobody noticed her sitting there, caught up as they were with coming and going. So, when a cowboy sitting on a bench across from her glanced her way more than once, she paid attention. He was rough looking, wore a belt buckle as big as a fist, cowboy boots that looked like they'd seen a few decades of mud and muck. She wondered what he found interesting about her, other than the possible ill intentions of a male.

He caught her eye again and when she glared, he looked away.

Crap, she thought, looking at her watch. She didn't like being gawked at and there was another hour before the north bound bus would arrive.

"Hey," he said.

"Hey," she said sarcastically.

"Don't mean to stare, don't mean nothing by it. But I was wondering where you got that duffle bag."

Dory looked at the beat-up gray bag. She'd always had it, never considered where it came from.

"I think it was my dad's, it's so old, but I don't really know. I'd have to ask my mom."

"Looks just like mine, is all," he spoke in an even tone that revealed nothing.

"Well, it's not yours. I've had it all my life." She didn't trust that all he was interested in was something so old and torn up.

"No, I still have mine. They don't make 'em like that anymore, so I just wondered where you got yours."

"From my dad, like I said."

"What was your dad's name?" he asked. She noticed he said "was."

"Burdine Hastings." She'd never met anyone who'd known her father, but this cowboy seemed about the right age, even looked a little like him. "You know him?"

"Yep," he said. His eyes dropped to the ground. "Where you off to?"

"Boot camp. Fort Leonard, Missouri."

"Wow, Missouri's a long way off."

"Nothing but dust for me in Biggs County," she said sourly and then asked, "How'd you know my dad?"

The question was lost as the space between them was suddenly choked with seventy or so passengers getting off a bus and filling the station.

The woman the man had been waiting on kissed him and grabbed him around the neck. She was pretty—long, dark hair with gray coming in at the temples, blue dangly earrings that matched her eyes. One of those families that hugged, Dory figured. He kept his arm around her shoulder while they waited for her suitcase to appear from beneath the bus, then walked together to a muddy truck parked nearby. He opened the passenger door for her and slung the suitcase in the back.

Then he walked back to where Dory was sitting. The woman in the car looked at Dory with a half-smile she found unnerving.

"Wouldn't mind a postcard if you get the chance," the cowboy said holding out a business card. Dory took the card and watched him get in the truck. He tipped his hat to her from behind the wheel, backed out and left.

She read the card, Jack Hastings, Owner. High Point Ranch, Biggs County FL.

It had never occurred to Dory that there might be more Hastings. She'd never heard of High Point Ranch. It struck her sad that no one but a stranger had asked her to send a postcard home. She pulled her wallet out of the duffle bag and placed the card in a slot where it would be safe.

The bus ride took thirty-one hours, long enough for Dory to question the wisdom of her plan. There'd be little privacy in boot camp and it worried her a bit. She stepped off the bus and was directed to a long green building with few windows.

Inside, a row of lockers lined one wall. Dory chose one and put her few personal things inside, a picture of Hank and Clara taken last Christmas, and the picture of her father. In the photo her father is smiling. Dory looked at the picture and believed she remembered that smile, even though he died when she was two. The photograph was her only proof that he even existed. She imagined, as she had imagined at various milestones throughout her life, that he was proud of her. She imagined that, as a soldier, he would see her as a hero, someone who placed the lives of others before her own. She tried to imagine his hand resting on her shoulder.

Women—girls, really—filed in through the afternoon and filled their lockers, stealing glances at each other. Finally, making introductions, the ice melted. They all stood in lines for hours at a time filling out paperwork and receiving vaccinations. The first few days were monotonous routines of waiting. As they waited, conversations sparked and friendships budded.

For Dory, used to her own bedroom and few friends, boot camp felt like coming home to a dormitory full of long-lost cousins. The daily exercise drained her; she found the training more interesting than she expected. She grew stronger and gained confidence. At night, the girls were exhausted and fell about the bunks sharing stories and pictures from home.

"Your dad was so handsome." Michelle, a strong-boned, brown-haired girl from Michigan whose parents divorced when she was thirteen, was practically moved to tears when she heard that Dory's dad had died so young. Dory liked Michelle. She was a no-nonsense, down-to-earth hard-ass.

"You probably don't even remember him," Michelle said. She had a habit of twisting a strand of hair when she spoke.

Lacy, blue-eyed and stocky, came from Alabama. Her southern drawl confounded Dory for a week.

"That Hank fella looks kinda like a groundhog," Lacy snickered, giving Dory a laugh. The picture was passed around and it was agreed; his face inspired the notion of some kind of tunneling varmint, though no one could pinpoint the exact species. They wondered why Clara had settled for a round and balding ex-preacher, a part-time wrestler turned car mechanic, after handsome Burdine. Dory admitted she couldn't figure it out and stuck the photo in the bottom of her duffle bag.

Lacy and Michelle accepted Dory at face value. They were baffled at Clara's disappointment in her, and didn't believe for a minute that her unplanned pregnancy had ruined Clara's life. They were outraged when Dory admitted she was sending her paycheck home, made her promise to cut that out straight away. "We watch each other's backs," they swore in allegiance, and Dory learned about loyalty. Soldiering and physical training wore her out every day, but during meals in the mess hall each evening, she learned to laugh a little more freely.

It was 2003 and the army was in need of soldiers to fortify the initial wave of the invasion. Despite the early claims of victory, the number of troops needed had been badly underestimated. At Fort Leonard, Dory's battalion, having successfully completed boot camp in six weeks, was propelled directly into logistical training. In three months, Dory was promoted to E-1 and deployed to Iraq. The work would keep her behind the lines in a materials handling regiment, its sole responsibility receiving and moving the supplies required to rebuild Iraq's bombed-out infrastructure.

Before she shipped out, she wrote to Clara, explaining that from now on she was going to have to keep her paychecks, as there were certain personal items she needed that the army didn't supply. She hoped Clara understood and wished them all well. When she finished the letter and dropped it in the post, she struggled through a moment of guilt. But she was going to the other side of the world with only a hundred dollars in her bank account and her next paycheck was two weeks away.

She also bought a postcard from the commissary and addressed it to Jack Hastings. She found it hard to know what to say to a stranger she'd met on her last day in Biggs County. In the end all she could think of was, "It was nice meeting you. How did you know my dad?" She signed it with her name and rank, thinking he'd probably already forgotten the meeting.

She stepped off the plane and was immediately grateful for the last-minute purchase of a pair of sunglasses from the commissary. The desert was a flare of blazing light, easily surpassing the glare of Florida. If she thought Biggs County was an empty, lifeless landscape, Iraq made it look like a paradise. She was there three months before the letter from Jack Hastings, forwarded from post to post for most of that time, finally arrived. Surprised to hear her name at mail call that morning, she stuck the letter inside her flak jacket to read at the end of the day's ride. It would be a long drive, eighty kilometers out and back, on thin roads that shifting sands covered over nearly every night. That day there was a convoy of four trucks. Dory rode in the last one.

She had strapped her helmet on just before the explosion. The Hummer tipped up on its front right in a hail of sand and yellow-gold flashes of fire. And then there was blackness. The only thing she remembered from the day was the color of the sand and fire; in total, three days were completely gone from her memory. When she finally opened her eyes, she was alone in a hospital bed, unable to move save her eyelids, and then only slightly. She could not know that her body, almost completely covered with shrapnel and third-degree burns, was wrapped in bandages. It was only minutes, though it felt like hours, before the attending medic, burdened with caring for a dozen injured soldiers, returned to her side. His eyes widened when he found her awake. "Can you hear me?" he mouthed. Slowly she understood that she couldn't and a swift wave of terror washed across her brain. The terror was soon relieved by another wave of unconsciousness brought on by the morphine dripping into an IV attached to her left arm. She'd been in Iraq three months and fourteen days.

Her left arm had been crushed under a dozen crates loaded with supplies. The surgeons had sewn it together, hoping to save it, but not knowing if it would ever work again. In a series of three operations, doctors repaired severed nerves, and bolted ligaments and bones together, in the hope that one day the arm would function near normal.

Her left leg was broken in two places. It healed slowly, requiring only one surgery, fewer bolts, and a succession of long hip-to-toes casts. Through all this, the most unnerving thing to Dory was the constant headache and the possibility of long-term brain damage.

Closed-head injuries, the doctors explained, were harder to diagnose. The anesthesia from the surgeries and the pain medication for the nerve damage complicated everything. Only time would tell. The smallest wounds, gashes from shrapnel and burns from flying metal in the initial explosion, healed long before she was deposited at Walter Reed. By then, another three months, spent mostly unconscious or knocked out by drugs, had passed. Her few possessions arrived a week after she did. Inside the small, neatly-packed carton, she found the letter from Jack Hastings, as yet unopened.

To Dory Hastings, U.S. Army, Fort Leonard, Missouri,

Let me begin by saying that I know this letter has been a long time coming. I don't know if I would have ever written you if I hadn't seen you sitting in the bus station that day back in June. I felt like I was seeing my brother in your face and plus you had that duffle bag. I knew it had to have been his. We each got one for Christmas way back when we were little kids. My wife, Brenda, the woman you saw me pick up that day, thought I should reach out to you. After giving it some thought, I had to agree. I've written this letter six times but keep throwing it away because it's so hard to put on paper what needs to be said. So, I'm sorry it took so long to get this in the mail to you.

Your daddy was my older brother, but I guess you won't remember me. You were still in diapers last time I saw you. We didn't understand why Burdine left Clara and you or what he was doing down in Key West. You could say there were some hard feelings between my folks and your mother. They blamed her for his leaving and for the changes in him. When he passed, my mom and dad had a bad time. They were heartbroken and they never got over it. After the funeral, they closed up his room and we never spoke his name again.

I was sixteen. I'd never known someone who died. I didn't know what to do with my grief. I quit school so I could spend more time outdoors. The only thing that seemed to help was keeping busy and there was always work on the ranch. We buried him in the family plot out in the back pasture, beneath an old oak tree. You can come see his marker any time you want. He's buried next to mom and dad as they have now passed away too.

That day at the bus station you said there was nothing for you in Biggs County but dust. But by rights part of this ranch belongs to you. My wife and I never had any kids of our own and there's plenty of room for you in this big old house. I'm mighty sorry that grief and senseless bitterness made me lose touch with you, but grateful that my brother left a part of himself in this world. I've sent along a picture of you and your dad sitting on the little black mare he got for his seventeenth birthday. The two of you were so happy that day. He loved that mare and I've kept her all these years. Thank you for the postcard. I hope you consider coming home to High Point Ranch when the Army lets you loose.

Sincerely,

Your Uncle, Jack Hastings.

When Dory stepped off the bus the sun was sinking low on the horizon of Biggs County. The familiar, flat landscape seemed almost welcoming. Her arm was in a cast and sling. There was an obvious limp in her gait but she carried herself without a cane. The travelers leaving the bus cut a considerate swath for the banged-up girl in the U.S. Army uniform. Jack and Brenda waited by the truck till she emerged from the crowd and then made their way to her side. The hugs were awkward, wary as they were of the arm in the cast, the hand that looked pale and withered. But the smile on Brenda's face, spreading from ear to ear and creasing the lines around her eyes, put Dory at ease.

Jack's expression was harder to read. He found it hard to speak, looked torn between a mournful grin and full-on tears. "We were so relieved when you sent word you'd decided to recuperate at High Point," he choked out and then fell silent as he drove.

They headed down Main Street, past the courthouse and the two short blocks lined with storefronts. Other than a few recently closed-up shops, everything seemed the same as always.

The road changed outside of town to a blacktop highway lined with white dashes and double yellow solid stripes. Speed markers and caution signs warned of sharp bends or soft shoulders. Brenda filled in the silence, chatting effortlessly about the fresh paint and new curtains in the room they'd spruced up for Dory.

After twenty minutes, the road forked and Jack let up on the gas. He veered left onto a gravel road. The truck bounced through some potholes but he avoided most of them, swerving from side to side.

"The county doesn't maintain private roads," Brenda offered as an apology. Dory held her cast tight to her chest to keep it from banging Jack's arm and said it wasn't hurting her. He slowed down some anyway.

Jacaranda trees in full purple bloom dotted the landscape. A smattering of cows grazed next to sleeping calves folded into the deep grass. Florida had to be the only state in the union where a thirty-foot rise above sea level could earn the name High Point, an observation that, Jack said, amused everyone who visited there.

Jack hauled her duffle bag up to the second floor and then excused himself to the barn, where the horses would need their water buckets filled. It was Brenda who took her to her the room, showed off the curtains she'd made, the shade of lemon yellow she'd chosen for the walls. Dory said it was a nice change from the dreary, colorless Army. Outside the window in the distance was an old oak tree surrounded by a sagging wrought iron fence. Dory guessed it was the family cemetery, shivered at the thought of how close she'd come to getting planted there herself.

"I'll let you settle in. That bus ride was long and you must be worn out. I set some water and a sandwich over there," Brenda said, pointing. "If you need anything else just call downstairs." She stepped through the door, reaching to close it behind her, and then paused. "By the way, your dad's old bedroom is the door across the hall. Just so you know."

Dory was grateful that Brenda had come to the station with Jack. She'd trusted her immediately, and decided that she was one of those rare women who had the gift of saying everything that needed to be said with a few words or a simple smile. Dory waited until she was sure Brenda was downstairs. Tired as she was, curiosity led her to the door across the hall.

The room was dimly lit in the fading glow of dusk. She was surprised by the sparse furnishings: a dresser, a bedside table, a desk, and a bed covered with an old, hand-sewn, red-and-white quilt. Bare wooden floors creaked with her every step. There was a poster from the 1973 Biggs County Fair tacked to the wall and next to that a blue ribbon that her dad won for the junior bull riding competition. The Stetson she'd seen him wearing in photographs hung on a high post of the headboard. Inside the headband was a thin line of sweat stain, evidence of hard work. She set it on her head, looked in the mirror over the dresser and thought it uncanny how much she looked like Burdine.

Photographs lined the top of the dresser and she searched them for faces she might recognize. An old man and woman standing next to an antique Model T-Ford—maybe her grandparents? A framed picture of young Clara and Burdine, dressed up and standing on the courthouse steps in the noon-day light. That must have been their wedding day; someone had reminded them to smile. A faded clipping from an old newspaper was taped to the mirror, her dad wearing that Stetson and riding a jet-black horse in a Fourth of July parade, alongside school pictures that spanned several years.

Stuck behind the others, a small snapshot in a wood frame caught her eye. She pulled it out and sat with it on the edge of the bed, catching the last of the light filtering through the window. Whoever took the picture had snapped it too soon, catching Burdine and Jack off guard. They weren't looking at the camera but at the child in their arms. Dory recognizes the child in the photograph as herself, maybe eighteen months old. A smiling Burdine, standing a foot taller than Jack, is handing the wiggling toddler to his little brother.

She stood the picture on the nightstand and picked up the old quilt her dad had slept beneath as a boy. She pressed the fabric, which had once touched his skin, to her face, hoping to sense something of him from all those years ago. Grateful for the unexpected solace, Dory wrapped the quilt around her body. She stretched out on the narrow bed, studying the photograph until the light faded. Tomorrow, she thought as night settled in the window, she would take an apple to the old black mare.

Swimaway

Pop would have my head if he knew that I had taken the hatchet upriver and smashed it against a boulder. He was a river man who kept his feet in mud and not the kind to understand sabotage. When I got back to camp, he was finishing a dugout canoe that he carved from the trunk of a cypress tree a hurricane had dropped on our beach last summer. It barely missed our storage shack and the lines in the clearing where we hung the bass to dry. Pop took it as a sign to make it into a boat. Every day for the past month, after we had strung up the fish caught overnight in our nets, he worked on the canoe. He used the hatchet's blade to hone the narrow bow and aft, and hollow out the middle. I made an oar out of driftwood and blades of swamp grass, thinking it was harmless fun. But he floated the canoe for the first time yesterday and I saw he was serious. I refused to help anymore and kept busy fixing my braids, gathering kindling, or pretending to nap. This morning I had hidden the hatchet under my skirt and took it upriver to bust it.

"It's almost done," he said when I returned in the afternoon. Pop dragged the sharp edge of a clam shell along the inside walls of the canoe, scraping and smoothing the remaining splinters from the wood.

I tossed the hatchet on the sand near the fire ring wishing I had busted it weeks ago. That canoe was meant to carry us away but this is the only home I've ever known. I built up the fire to heat water for a tea of berries and sassafras. Pop doesn't eat anymore and he's too thin, so I lace his with teaspoonfuls of sugar.

"What happened to that?" he asked when he saw the broken hatchet half-buried in the sand next to the fire.

I shrugged. "The straps finally wore out, I guess."

Pop ran his hand along the smooth inside of the hull, his arms and elbows like knotted twigs. "She's almost finished."

A dragonfly buzzed around my head and landed on my knee. I waited, as still as a stone, until it closed its eyes, then grabbed it, peeled off its wings, and tossed it on the grill. Dragonflies are tasty when slightly charred but the wings are flavorless dust on my tongue. I ignored its screams. Pop hummed and covered his ears.

He drank his tea while the sounds of crickets and night birds surrounded us. Fireflies lit the opposite shore. I waited for Pop to fall asleep then dragged the canoe to the fire, but the cypress had fallen when it was young and its flesh was too moist to burn. The flames blackened a small spot near the bow but then the wind changed direction and the spark never took.

"Accidents happen." He examined the black smudge on the canoe the next morning. "It would take a bonfire as big as this beach for her to catch." I glared at the fire, feigning relief, letting him keep his own lie.

We were known to the bands of traders who came by our camp to barter for dried fish. They appeared on our shore randomly throughout the seasons. Some returned, some we only saw once. Trappers, snake charmers, alligator hunters. They offered goods or services. Some came begging for whatever we could give in exchange for river gossip. Once, Pop paid an astrologer who told him I was a water sign, and a palm reader who said I belonged to the river. A banjo player spent a week with us and taught me to yodel at the moon. Last year, when Pop was off in the woods, an old hag paddled to our shore. I traded her a basket of fish for some licorice and a string of shiny beads. She pushed off in her raft laughing as Pop returned to the campfire. He threw rocks at her raft, water splashing in her wake like shards of glass. "People steal children out here. Did she give you candy?"

I showed him the beads but kept the licorice in my pocket until I was able to hide it in my secret place inside the shack.

～

That evening a floating band of evangelicals drifted downriver, singing their hymns. They saw our campfire and called out. Pop was excited for company. He waved them to the stump where they tied up their barge. When they waded to shore, I moved to the edge of the forest like he taught me to do when I was little. Their faces were long and shadowy with intermittent maniacal smiles.

I should have stayed hiding, but Pop was a terrible negotiator and he'd be taken for everything we had, even the broken hatchet, and we'd get nothing in return. Not even licorice.

Their leader was called Preacher and he dressed in rags. In a few moments I knew I was right, that all they had to trade were bible stories. They spread out around the campfire with their blankets and hogged all its warmth. But Pop loved stories. He threw more logs on the fire, and turned the canoe upside down to accommodate them.

His obsession with the canoe had made him sullen, but the evangelicals revived him. His eyes brightened; his cheeks turned pink. They built more fires, lit up the entire beach, and told stories of Noah's ark and the flood, of snakes and a forbidden fruit. They took their stories from an old black book and ignored the ancient battles recorded in stars wheeling through the sky every night.

There was no space for me next to Pop, so I went inside the shack. Away from the river, its mineral smell and the sound of lapping water, I slept in restless spells, soothing myself with strings of licorice. Near morning, I peeked out the doorway. The fire had died out and slumbering mounds of evangelicals were scattered along the beach. Pop and the Preacher sat by the dying embers huddled under blankets, praying. It made me unreasonably angry and my skin flashed hot. Pop never prayed except to implore the river to share more of its fish.

Pop came to the shack and poked his head. "Wake up, Punkin." That was his name for me when he was happy. I sat up and pretended to rub sleep from my eyes. "Preacher is baptizing us today. Bring out all the fish we have stored. It's a celebration."

I couldn't even count the number of evangelicals on the beach. Dozens, I think because I've only ever counted in dozens. Three, maybe four. "We don't have enough to feed all these people." It wasn't true. We had enough to feed them for weeks.

"We have plenty." He scowled at me through a darkening mood. "And they are our guests."

"We don't need guests," I said and threw myself back onto my cot. "They have nothing to trade."

He took my shoulder in his big hand and squeezed which surprised me because he'd always been gentle. "Punkin, I've been waiting years for them to come. We need to be baptized. Both of us."

With the sunlight behind his head his face seemed like a skull. I was hot again but this time it wasn't anger I felt. He loosened his grip and my shoulder went cold.

The women laid out white tablecloths on the beach, pinned them down with their shoes, and set out platters of food. They hid their hair under bandanas and wore long skirts that dragged in the sand. Streams of sweat poured off their chins, but they didn't complain about the sun beating down from the clean blue sky. I wiped my forehead with my shirt and one of them gave me a disapproving glance. She found a handkerchief in the folds of her skirt and using it to wipe her face showing off the manners of her people, but my people are of the river and manners have never served us. Yellow-eyed Grackles danced near the platters of fish that me and Pop pulled from the river with our nets. The fish we spent months of hard work stringing up, drying, and storing. I threw pebbles at the birds to keep them from stealing our meal.

Preacher prayed over the food but I was already crunching a mouth full of fish bones and besides, it was all mumbo-jumbo. Pop caught me mid-chew, but the prayer ended before I could swallow. A bone got stuck in my throat and made me feel like a little kid until I went behind the shack and coughed it up. After lunch Pop called me over. Preacher waded waist-deep into the water. I stood tucked next to Pop's side on the shore, his arm tight around my waist. Preacher bowed in the four directions then motioned to us. Pop waded out quietly and let Preacher dunk him backwards in the water. It looked harmless but now his clothes were soaking and he was too skinny to catch a frivolous chill. The evangelicals hooted and clapped and the Grackles lifted all at once and flew into the pines. The sun was scalding my head. Pop waved me out to join them.

Preacher pulled me to stand in front of him. A school of minnows nibbled at my toes. The evangelicals sang their hymns. Grackles screeched. Preacher mumbled his prayers.

"Water brings rebirth," Preacher said, and pushed me under.

Salvation was the still quiet below the surface. Through the prism of water Pop elongated and morphed into a stranger. I twisted out of Preacher's grip.

I swam away to where the river ran wide. On impulse I breathed in. Slits opened along my ribcage. Water became air. Webbing emerged between my fingers and toes. Blue-green scales flashed on my forearms.

Across the river everyone was wading to shore. With any luck the evangelicals would leave soon. Let them fill their baskets if they want. The river held more than we would ever need.

Bass as long as my arm swam beside me. Deep below the surface a spring surged from between ancient boulders hiding the entrance to a cave. I swam into it. Sunlight filtered through an above ground opening. Mastodon bones were strewn across the floor. Catfish as big as a child's body hovered near the bottom. I found a ledge, climbed out of the water to dry, and my body returned to its previous human state. The webbing between my toes contracted as my gills folded into a ribcage and the scales on my arms fell away.

~

In the morning the evangelicals loaded their rafts with the rest of our baskets of fish and thanked Pop for his generosity. Preacher wanted to spread his good news to a wider congregation he'd heard about down south. He asked Pop and me to join them but I shook my head no.

Pop's skin was yellow again. The cheekbones jutting from his face. A breeze lifted his thin hair off his forehead. He flipped the canoe upright. "You need new clothes," he said. "And we can't wait for people to drift by hoping they'll bring what we need."

The evangelicals pushed away from shore. Preacher smiled at Pop. "You coming, Brother?"

Brother. Pop started to lift his hand but the word wounded him. A word that held so little meaning to me seemed his only cure.

I dragged the canoe off the beach and held it steady. "Get in."

Pop nodded.

"I'll find you later," I said. It might have been true. Anytime I wanted I could catch a ride on a trader's raft.

Downstream, the evangelicals navigated a bend in the river.

Pop climbed in and sat cross-legged in the hull. He tested the oar and I pushed the canoe farther out. It glided effortlessly through the water.

"She rides even," I said, wading beside the canoe, pushing it into the current.

Sunlight glinted on the surface as he paddled silently downstream and disappeared around the last bend. Grackles lifted from the trees and returned to my beach. A breeze blew across the river invoking that intoxicating smell. My gills flared and my fingers and toes twitched. My arms flashed blue-green.

Marked

Callie stood at home plate in the first inning of the game hoping for the right pitch when she heard the crash. A breeze rustled the palm trees out past the left field fence. Overhead the sunset had turned the sky purple. The crowd in the bleachers went silent waiting for the metal against metal screech to stop, but it went on so long that everyone knew it had been deadly. The dugout emptied onto the field, the players and coaches stood facing south where the train crossed Park Boulevard even though that intersection was a quarter mile away and blocked from view by city hall and none of them could see a thing. Pinellas Park had been built after the railroad and the tracks ran through the small town at a foolish angle. Callie rested the bat on her shoulder and scrunched up her face, but that thing people talk about, how you know in your gut someone close to you has died? That part never happened. After the game resumed, the lights on the field came on, she swung at a fast ball, and struck out. By the last inning her granddad had arrived to tell her the news.

It never dawned on her that her parents might've been in that car. They had said they wanted a few minutes alone and dropped her off at the field promising to be right back. It seemed they were always trying to get a few minutes to themselves, a thing she doesn't understand even now, two years later. The three of them were always happy enough, riding in the pick-up with Callie squeezed between them, her father's arm stretched behind her back, playing with a lock of her mother's hair.

Burial expenses wiped out the equity on their small cinderblock house so it went back to the bank. Her granddad, the town's widowed preacher, insisted on a four-foot-tall family headstone, had it installed beneath the ancient moss-draped oak at the grave of his long-dead wife, and bought two silk-lined mahogany caskets. Nothing less, he claimed, would serve the memory of his son. Callie saw the reasoning there but when Granddad paid for three plots, one for each of her parents and one for himself, it bothered her. The old man explained that when she grew up, she'd have a husband and when she died, she'd have to be buried next to him, but it was a man and a situation Callie already knew would never exist.

On the day of the funeral the crowded church was sweltering beneath the Florida sun. Halfway through delivering his son's eulogy, her granddad had a stroke that nearly killed him. He never walked again and soon his ability to speak vanished. He went into the retirement home two blocks from the high school and Callie went into a foster care group home. But in a town that was Little League crazy, the half-grown girl never got noticed by families looking to adopt.

The sudden upheaval in her life was a shock, but a well-meaning counselor at family services stepped in to teach her how to manage the anxiety that had begun consuming her. The better help came from a large bottle of small blue pills that the house manager gave her at intervals throughout the day and anytime she asked for another. The pills helped her breathe on bad days. On other days they kept her from biting her nails to the quick. The first year after the train wreck passed without lodging itself in her memory. She went through the motions of brushing her teeth and eating but her mind was always at home plate, the bat resting on her shoulder, listening to the screeching metal.

With help from the pills two years crept by so slowly that her memory felt like she was watching a movie about some other girl and some other family. After another year Callie couldn't trace herself back to a moment when she wasn't sliding toward panic. Approaching a window caused a small jolt of adrenaline to burst inside her stomach. A door could leave her paralyzed. The house manager kept an eye on her, took her shopping sometimes at the Dollar Store at the strip center in town just for the distraction of stocking up on household goods. Callie hated shopping. The store added dimension to the world when what she craved was something that would make it smaller. Shelf after shelf of canned and boxed food. Where did it all come from? Who had touched it? Had they washed their hands? Everyone knew about tampering, how it happened all the time.

Opening jars was the worst. Wondering what some stranger might have put in the applesauce or toothpaste. Anything could be tainted, especially Dollar Store products where the poor people shopped, but the house manager refused to waste money across town at the more expensive Winn-Dixie. Callie stayed awake at night worrying that the food from supper had been contaminated by a disgruntled worker on a production line, amused at the thought of killing a stranger on the other side of the country. Callie took to slitting the tube to get the toothpaste out of the bottom. She'd use it a few times and throw it out, count herself lucky each time she survived. Eventually she stopped using it altogether because the counselor told her it was good to trust her intuition and her intuition made her suspicious of Dollar Store toothpaste.

On the really bad days, when even four pills didn't help, she used matches. She kept a pack with her because somedays just holding the matchbook was enough, on other days the smell of sulfur was enough. On really bad days she had to feel the burn. The burn turned her mind white. It told her she was strong and had nothing to hide from because in the middle of a burn the only choice was to endure.

A girl at school had asked if she wanted to see a match burn twice and Callie had been intrigued. The girl struck the match, blew it out, and touched it to Callie's arm. She screamed as white light exploded behind her eyes.

The girl laughed and said, "Make your mark or the world will make it on you."

Callie saw her point. Right then she decided to make her own marks—a strip of burn scars down the inside of her arm.

The burn hit the back of her head first and wiped her mind clean. Nothing else existed while her head was lit up like that. The counselor noticed the scars. She made a note on Callie's chart and suggested she trade softball for basketball. The next day a new prescription showed up and was added to her morning medication. Callie studied the new pill. It was solid and harder to swallow and sometimes got lodged sideways in her throat and hurt until it dissolved.

Basketball was no more fun than softball. She couldn't run and dribble at the same time, she always got turned around on the floor and ran to the wrong net, but she was taller than the other girls and able to snag rebounds over their heads. The coach told her to plant herself under their net and stay there. It was a losing season and the coach cut her after the last game. The counselor told her sports weren't for everyone and signed her up for the junior ROTC in the hope that she might develop responsibility and leadership skills, maybe start to see a future for herself beyond graduation.

Officer Sloan ran the Junior ROTC program at the high school. There was a rumor that he wrestled for money at the armory on Saturday nights and she felt safer when he was around because no one was fool enough to start a fight in his presence. Halfway through the second semester he started taking the class to the shooting range to teach gun safety and get them some target practice.

The first time she held a gun she was surprised at its weight. The heft of it sent a charge up her arm all the way to the center of her stomach. The feeling didn't have a name but as she stood there turning the gun over in her hand, she felt a shift inside.

Sloan came up behind her. "It feels good, right?" he asked.

It did feel good.

"The rules are simple. Keep the barrel aimed at the floor and never point it at anything you don't mean to destroy," he said.

He showed her how to open the cylinder and load the bullets. One by one she slid them into place then flipped the cylinder closed. He took the gun and handed her ear muffs, pointed the pistol toward the target, and fired off a round.

She watched him, the twitch in his shoulder. The bullets shredded the paper target at the end of their lane.

"Now you," he said and she reloaded.

He stepped behind her, adjusted her grip, and put his hand on the back of her right shoulder blade. She shuddered. It was the most human contact she'd had since sitting on her father's lap in church.

Sloan didn't notice. "You're going to feel the kick right here. Brace for it and pull the trigger."

When she fired, his hand caught the kick in her shoulder. The bullet tore a hole near the center of the target.

"I knew it," he said. "You're a natural."

He stepped back and she emptied the cylinder. It was like a wind sweeping through her bones. The gun was hot in her hand, her breath steady and even. Her spine straightened as though tempered by the strength of metal. Guns cracked all around her, up and down the firing lanes, and left an intoxicating smell in the air.

She got a part-time job at the range just to be near that noise, smell that smell. For the first time in her life she didn't mind waking early. One hour before school to empty the bins of shredded paper targets and sweep the lanes of used casings, saving the last ten minutes for practice. The rush from shredding a paper human was the medicine she needed most. Her first paycheck surprised her. She would have done it for free. She bought a necklace at the strip mall, a bullet on a chain that once she put on, she never took off again. Her enthusiasm pleased Sloan and earned her the honor of packing up the pistols and carrying them to the backseat of his apple red truck each Friday after class ended.

Scared. She'd felt scared for as long as she could remember, but pulling that trigger made everything different. Holding a gun calmed her more than the pills, more than the breathing techniques the counselor had taught her, more than the match-head on her skin. She didn't need to burn anymore and the counselor took that as a sign of progress. The weight of the gun, the smell, and the blast, annihilated fear, squashed and contained it to a size she imagined small enough to fit inside the bullet she wore around her neck.

The bullet was a touchstone that she reached for each morning. A totem, a solid thing to hold onto when so much else seemed vague. She held it in her hand whenever she heard the train pass through town, remembering the terrible noise from the wreck, knowing it had been a curse for her parents to die with that noise all around them. She drew strength from the bullet on her way to school, as she walked down Park Boulevard past the Feed and Seed, the small white church with its high steeple, and the motel where the drunks sat on the curb, so close she could smell the whiskey on their breath. The bullet gave her the strength to jog until the air smelled clean again. She touched it as she walked through the lunch room trying to find an empty table where she could eat her bag lunch alone, when she left the school grounds in the afternoon, and at night when she crawled in bed. Her fingers were wrapped around the bullet when she closed her eyes and the last pill entered her bloodstream, traveled to her brain, and allowed her mind to go dark for a few hours.

She was dreaming of her granddad when she woke on Friday morning. She knew he'd been in the Army years ago, that he would be proud of her aim, and the skill she had in handling a pistol. After class she loaded Sloan's truck with the gun cases. He'd parked behind a stand of palmetto bushes which made it easy to hide while she slipped the smallest revolver from its case and stuffed it in her backpack.

Alone behind the gun range she loaded the bullets she'd stolen from Sloan's truck. She spun the cylinder a few times, feeling the metal's satisfying clicks, snapped it closed. The weight of cold steel resting in her hands, the power she felt stirring in her gut. It made no sense how much she loved having this thing all to herself. She touched the bullet hanging around her neck remembering her father's wedding band and how she would play with it on Sundays while listening to her granddad preach. The church was hot on those mornings. Air conditioning wasn't in the budget and the windows were too high up for a decent cross breeze, but it wasn't considered Christianly to complain. Before the heat pulled her into a stupefying sleep she would sit on her father's lap and play with his ring. His hands were big, the ring too small to slip over his knuckles but she would try until her eyelids grew too heavy.

She thought about waking up in church with her father's arm draped over her shoulder as she walked to the retirement home. The old man had aged fast and seemed to be caving in on himself more each week. After his stroke they kept him strapped in a wheelchair, his head bobbing, drool spilling on the pajamas he wore all the time. He never talked but moaned often and loudly. He was on the front porch when she arrived, watching an egret over by the Oleanders stalk its supper. It stabbed a lizard and ran to the edge of the grass.

The pill she was supposed to have taken at lunch was still in her pocket. She popped it in her mouth and chewed it to make the calm come faster.

She showed him the bullet on its chain. He nodded and it seemed he understood. She wiped the drool off his chin with the blanket draped across his lap. She told him she brought the gun to show him, that it was inside her backpack.

He grabbed her hand and she was surprised at his strength. He knocked her hand against his sternum, mouthed the word, "Here."

"Yes," she said. "I have it here."

She told him how anytime she touched the bullet she felt better.

His hand dropped to his knee and waved like a dying fish, perturbed, uneasy. A squirrel came onto the porch, sniffing around for the peanuts the staff set out every afternoon. Callie hated squirrels, thought of them as rodents with fluffy tails. She kicked at it and it jumped into the grass.

"Me," he said.

"What?"

He grabbed her hand and placed it over his heart. "Right here."

A red truck pulled into the parking lot and she thought briefly of how almost everyone in town had a relative in this place.

It was the first time her granddad had touched her in years but now she understood. She'd taken the gun for one reason, loaded it for one reason.

She slung her backpack over her shoulder and wheeled him back inside, through the dining hall where the staff was putting out fresh bibs and juice boxes, down a corridor of rooms with noisy televisions, passed the aide at the medicine cart, and the janitor mopping the tiled floor.

She got her granddad inside his room and locked the door.

The gun was wrapped in a hand towel inside her backpack. When she unwrapped it and showed it to him his eyes turned bright. He spoke some mumbled words that might've been a prayer. She took it as a sign. He was rocking back and forth. He was excited but so was she.

Someone tried to open the door and her granddad hushed. The handle jerked a few more times then stopped.

He tapped his chest and mumbled more things she couldn't understand.

Red lights hit the window pane. Another ambulance, another resident, another old-timer with a stopped heart. He stared out the window briefly then looked back at her. She brought the pistol close to him. He reached for it and knocked it out of her hand.

It was disgusting having to put her hands on the floor under his bed, guessing at the kind of germs that were sticking to her palms. The pistol had slid next to some half-eaten toast and a ball of used tissue. She grabbed the gun and crawled out from under the bed.

She understood this was scary for him, but she knew what was right. She had aim. She had this one skill. She was a natural. Then she had a moment of doubt. Maybe he didn't understand. Maybe waving his hand like that meant something else entirely. Maybe she had it all wrong.

A voice shouted from the hallway. Someone banged on the door.

There was always doubt before she swung at the ball, before she lit the match, doubt before swallowing a pill. She knew not to give into doubt. She had intuition. When it came down to it, she had follow-through.

She put the pistol to her granddad's chest, took a deep breath.

The blast knocked her against the wall. She slid to the floor wondering how there'd been so much kick. Maybe she hadn't planted her feet. Maybe the gun had misfired.

The window was blown out, her granddad still sat upright in his wheelchair, the floor and his lap covered in shattered glass.

Sloan stood outside the window, so close he could have stepped into the room, his mouth set in a hard line. He kept her gaze, kept the rifle pointed at her as the janitor swung open the door. Sloan lowered the gun and said, "The rules were easy, Callie."

The bullet, lodged somewhere in her lungs, spread a dull ache down each arm, up into her head, throughout her torso. The cold dead weight of the pistol sat in her hand and she tried to close her fingers around it. It was impossible to move, to reach for the bullet hanging around her neck. She heard the train approach, saw a mound of shredded paper targets in its path, endured the searing pain. Then, as air of her final breath escaped through the hole in her chest Callie saw herself standing at home plate, the bat resting on her shoulder, hoping for the right pitch.

Ivy Waters

Whether it was the moonlight suddenly flooding her bedroom or the fleeting image of a dream or the urgency of her mother's voice in the living room that woke her, Ivy would never know. What she felt, lying in the half-light, was a brief premonition of loss.

A night breeze lifted the curtains in the window but did nothing to cool the air in the house. Sweat coated her skin even at midnight, even with the sheet kicked aside. Ivy stepped into the darkened hallway where her parents' voices floated on the warm air. She sat with her back against the wall, cooling her bare legs on the terrazzo floor, and listened.

Sometimes Hank and Ruby told each other about their day. Their words revealed things, like whether or not his paycheck would cover the bills, if she was happy with her children, or if their troubled son had made any progress at school. Often, they repeated the old family stories, like how he'd lost his eye in "the war," how old Frankie was before they knew something was wrong with his brain, stories Ivy had heard all her life. There were times when she learned things she regretted knowing, but she seized every detail—she wanted the facts that came only after she and Frankie had gone to bed and her parents had taken their places on the couch in the living room of their small cinder block house.

The old window unit whined with a sporadic and useless effort, barely moving the air at all. Its motor groaned, metal against metal, sometimes muting her father's words but not their meaning. In between the noise and the quiet he spoke of the surgeon he'd seen that day at the veteran's hospital. "They have to operate," he said. "I can't put it off any longer."

Ivy caught her breath and peered around the corner.

"When?" Ruby asked.

"Soon," he said. "They'll call when they have an opening."

Her mother's voice tightened. She let out a high-pitched "no," but it sounded more like a moan than a word. Crying was not her mother's way and the sound of it worried the girl. Ruby Waters considered her face to be her best attribute and always said that crying made your eyes swell, and that it never put anything right, so you might as well swallow your tears and put on a smile. That night, though, she covered her mouth with her hand and buried her face against her husband's chest, her brown hair falling across his undershirt.

Ivy expected her father to respond, to find the words that would put the world back in order. But he simply patted Ruby's back and stared at the ceiling. His dejected face and her mother's quiet sobbing confused Ivy and made heat build behind her eyes. She pushed her forehead against the cold wall to freeze her own tears before they could escape, and then she went back to bed and pulled the sheet over her head, hoping sleep would come quickly.

The next morning her father hitched the bass boat to the back of the old 57' Oldsmobile while her mother packed the trunk. They took their usual places in the car and drove out of the carefully planned grid of their neighborhood of quarter acre lots and pastel houses of yellow and blue that Ivy imagined, from the sky, looked like a giant hand-sewn quilt. On Central Avenue they drove past the church, the high school, and the old dime store that sat across from the baseball field. At the edge of town, after the last stop light and the new two-story Sears building, the road merged with the county highway, curved slightly and ran north toward the river.

The rear end of their car sat low to the road, weighed down by the tackle box, a cooler packed with Cokes and ice, and the strain of towing the boat. Frankie stared out the window, his transistor radio pressed to his ear, muttering baseball scores under his breath. Ivy sat next to him, in the middle of the backseat, watching the road pass by out the window.

She had such a sense of contentment as the view shifted from scraggly wooded pines to yellow fields and back to woods that she wondered if she'd heard her father correctly the night before. Riding in the backseat of the car, with her family so close, it was hard to believe anything as large as surgery loomed over the future.

The wind whipped through the open car windows, cooling the sweat from her skin. Her father stopped his canvas fishing hat from blowing off and tugged it down. His hat was old and frayed and needed to be replaced, but he wore it every time he went fishing and kept his best lures pinned on the brim. With one hand on the wheel, he flung his other arm across the back of the seat to play with a strand of his wife's hair. At his touch, Ruby smiled though her eyes remained hidden behind black sunglasses. "Honey, you sure are pretty," he said, taking his good eye off the road and glancing at her.

The morning light bounced off the hood of the car so that Ivy had to shield her eyes. It was only nine o'clock and heat already rose off the blacktop in waves. The road sloped down from the middle into ditches so that in a rainstorm it wouldn't flood, but it hadn't rained for weeks and the ditches were lined with dry grass.

Ruby fanned herself with a section of the newspaper and peered through the windshield at the sky. "I wish it would rain."

Hank grinned. "One day it got so hot that the tar melted and slid right off the road."

"Funny," her mother said, not laughing.

"You're making that up, Dad." Ivy thought of the road workers scraping tar out of the ditch and shoveling it back onto the road and was glad her father was a carpenter because she loved how he smelled of fresh sawdust when he came home from work and she hated the smell of tar. There was a girl in homeroom whose father worked the roads and Ivy smelled it on the girl's clothes all the time.

The wind caught Hank's hat again and he tugged it hard. He glanced in the rearview mirror. The weight he'd lost showed in his face. Even the dark circles beneath his eyes and the crook in his nose seemed bigger. "Girl, you look more like your mama every day," he said.

Ivy felt her mother bristle. It happened every time her father pointed out the resemblance between his wife and his daughter. She considered the possibility that she was her mother's twin and decided it was unlikely. An event like that could have only been caused by a miracle like the birth of Jesus, or man walking on the moon, or the parting of the Red Sea. It was true, though. Ivy was in many ways a duplicate of her mother. Ruby's childhood pictures, the few that had survived the years, confirmed it. They both had that stick straight hair and grayish eyes that caught too much light and caused excessive squinting. Frankie, though, he had his father's dark eyes and the same bend in his nose.

"It's the eyes," he continued. "You could be her double."

A fly buzzed against the windshield. Ruby rolled up the newspaper and swatted at it. "Oh. Just fly out the window, for Pete's sake," she said.

A cloud, big as a mountain, filled the eastern horizon and Ivy worried that the drought might break before they got to the river. If a cloud that big split in two it would cause a thunderstorm. Thunder would wreck Frankie's nerves and put the whole day in jeopardy. She prayed that the cloud would blow south or hold itself together for another hour. It would only take one bolt of lightning across the sky for her mother to change her mind and issue the order to turn the car around.

A few miles later, they swerved onto the dusty service road that led to the river, passing around potholes and washed-out boulders. At the end, where the road widened into a turnout, the river came into view, a clean slice against the forest shadow. Her father backed the trailer down the ramp, unlatched the hitch, and let the boat slip into the crystal blue vein that sprung from Florida's limestone bedrock and ran west to the Gulf of Mexico.

Ivy sat cross-legged on the bow, keeping an eye out for cypress roots and shallows as they motored down river. The spring water ran clear as air. Black-eyed fish darted into underwater crevices. A Great Blue Heron flew upstream, lifting at the last moment right over their heads. Breaking light filtered between the branches of trees draped thick with moss.

Hank tied Frankie's life vest with double knots, turned his radio off, and told him to stay in his seat. Frankie sat stiff as a board looking warily at the river, his intense eyes staring out from beneath his ball cap. He checked his watch now and again, as though there was somewhere he needed to be.

Ruby leaned against a pile of life vests in the back of the boat, her face tilted toward the sun. In her black bathing suit and sunglasses, she looked like a movie star. Every couple of minutes Hank turned around to look at her.

At their favorite beach Hank tossed the anchor overboard and pulled off his sweatshirt. Stripped down to his swimming trunks, it was clear that his flesh had withered, his elbows grown knobby. The sight of his rib cage showing through his skin made Ivy flinch.

"There's no finer thing in the world than a spring-fed river," he said, and jumped off the back of the boat. Ivy was right behind him, smacking the water with a cannonball. The cold water hitting every inch of her skin took her breath away, but she didn't care. It was beautiful below the surface. An underwater spring flowed from between slats of limestone. She swallowed mouthfuls of it. This is what she'd come for, water so rich in minerals her body sometimes ached just for the smell of it. Her love for the river moved through her bloodstream. She swam into the current and felt its force push her back to the surface. If only she could sprout gills, breathe water like air, if only she could soar with the twitch of a fin, rise with the push of a tail. She imagined herself a fish—a carp, a catfish, an eel.

She kicked against the water until she was chilled through to the bone, her lips blue, her teeth chattering. Her mother yelled, "Ivy, get out of that water before you go numb and drown."

Only then did she climb onto the shore, wrap a quilt around her body, and find a place on the beach where the sun had warmed the sand. Light filtered through overhead branches. An occasional breeze rippled across the water, rustled through the woods. The world was silent except for the random caw-caw of a crow. It might have been the Garden of Eden. They might have been the first family.

Her father got the tackle box and carried it to shore. Inside it was lined with careful rows of lures—alderflies, beetles, red and blue damselflies—tiny steel hooks wrapped with thread and feathers. He tied his own. He chose yellow dragonflies and green scuds, good for early spring, and pinned them to the brim of his hat. He picked his way over the uneven stone bed and waded upriver. Nothing made him smile as big as a wide-mouth bass leaping into the air to chase a hand-tied bug. Further upstream, where the river widened, he cast his line across the surface, let it dance for an instant over the water, and then swept it up over his head behind him and out again in a widening arc.

Ivy watched him from the shore. At twelve years she still believed that plucking a bass from the water was half luck, half magic. He'd taught her everything he knew about fishing but she was still too small to cast a fly rod. She thought about asking him to let her try but decided not to pester him. The river calmed him in a way that nothing else could. It calmed her too.

"Don't just sit there. Get me some kindling," Ruby said as she cleared the ashes from an old fire ring. Once Hank caught enough fish, her mother would skewer them and cook them over hot coals.

Ivy took Frankie by the hand and led him to the edge of the woods where patches of wild berries grew. She'd caught up with him in height but he still outweighed her by twenty pounds. He held his arms out in front of him, bent at the elbow, as Ivy gathered sticks. He hated the itch of the splintery wood on his skin, but they'd done this before and he would tolerate it for a while.

Frankie had a low startle point and her parents often took pains to explain things to him that they simply didn't bother to tell Ivy. Often, he knew more than she did about the state of affairs at home like why their father hardly ate anymore and why he was always going off to see the doctor.

She lowered her voice and said, "I wonder what's wrong with Daddy."

"D-Daddy? Nothing's wrong with Daddy."

The kindling teetered in his arms but Ivy steadied him with her hand on his shoulder. She was certain he knew something. "Did they tell you about the operation?"

His voice grew louder. "Nothing's wrong with Daddy." He lowered his arms and the kindling fell to the ground. "Nothing's wrong."

"Shhh! Calm down." She glanced toward the clearing, gathering the sticks at his feet. "Mama will hear you."

But it was too late. Ruby walked into the woods and glared at her daughter. "What's going on here?"

Frankie rubbed the debris off his arms. "Nothing's wrong with Daddy," he said. His voice twisted an octave higher.

"What did you say to him?"

"I didn't say anything." Ivy tried to hand Frankie the kindling but he waved her off. "He dropped the wood, is all."

"Well, pick it up."

"Mama said he's fine," Frankie said. His back stiffened and his hands shook. His mother wrapped her arms around him anyway and rocked him against her chest. She was the only person in the world who could get away with touching him during a fit.

"Frankie, calm down and listen to me." She changed her tone and soothed him in a sweet, sing-song voice, a tone that she usually reserved for the men of the family. Years ago, when Ivy was a little girl, her mother sometimes used that voice to calm her after a nightmare.

It took a while but Frankie settled down. Ruby led him back to the water's edge where he could listen to the radio and see his father as he fished upstream. Ivy carried the wood to the fire ring.

Ruby struck a match and lit a handful of dry grass. "You know better than to upset him."

Ivy nudged a stone with her toe to push it in line with the others.

"Don't touch that," Ruby snapped.

Ivy picked out a heavy stick to use as a poker because even if her mother started every sentence with the word don't, it would be up to her to put out the fire if Frankie caused another distraction.

"Is Dad okay?"

Ruby fanned the small blaze with a sprig of pine needles. "I hope so," she said and looked toward the river. "I sure hope so."

As Ivy watched the lines in her mother's face shift from annoyance to worry, she tried to imagine the world without her father. Who would protect Frankie from the boys who made fun of him at church? How would Ivy get along with her mother, without her father's constant interventions? There was her cousin, Walter, who was barely out of high school, and her grandfather, but he never came around. Her father was their anchor. He was all that kept them from spinning into space.

Hank stood hip deep in the water, light shimmering off the ripples. Kindling crackled in the fire, sending up a small spiral of smoke. Ivy crossed her fingers and repeated her mother's words under her breath, "I hope so too."

Frankie watched Hank from the shore, grumbling about the possible safety hazards of standing too long in seventy-two-degree water but mostly quiet, because even out here, in the middle of nowhere, he could still hear the baseball game on his transistor radio. "Batter up!" he shouted, jabbing the air with his finger, and Ivy knew that somewhere along the eastern coast of the United States, a baseball game had started.

It was after sunset by the time they got home, the sky fading and the crickets just beginning their night song. Hank and Ruby went straight to the living room. He rested in his easy chair and she stretched out on the couch. They listened to the evening news, while Ivy unloaded the car and

Frankie washed the camping dishes.

The clock ticking on the window ledge over the sink was loud with a constant rhythm that made evening chores hypnotic and familiar. Frankie's mouth twitched as he counted the ticks. Ivy knew he'd want to get the job done on time, not one second early and not one second late.

She stood against the back door, watching while he finished rinsing. His fingers were pink from the scalding water.

"That's enough, Frankie."

He picked up the yellow checked kitchen towel and dried his hands.

"Not so hard or you'll scrub them raw."

As he stood at the sink drying his hands, Frankie counted the seconds under his breath. "Five hundred ninety-nine." He stopped counting, laid the towel on the kitchen table, folded it in half and smoothed its wrinkles. "Three-hundred-and-forty-eight yellow checks, sixty-four cut in half at the fold, and three-hundred-and-sixty white checks," he said. He picked up his watch and strapped it on his wrist. "Timex. It takes a licking and keeps on ticking."

Ivy understood Frankie better than she understood herself. He liked numbers and the color yellow but he hated wrinkles and took every opportunity to flatten them. He ironed the kitchen towel every night after drying the dishes. He loved ironing and soapy water, but hated most everything else, and if he hated something, that was the end of it. Try and make him do it and he'd pitch a fit. Ask him to wash the Oldsmobile and he'd run get a bucket but ask him to spread peanut butter on a piece of bread and he'd storm out of the house. Ivy had memorized a list of acceptable chores and always made sure to use the yellow kitchen towels.

Frankie smoothed the towel one last time and went out to the living room.

Ivy went out to the backyard. The air grew damp and heavy as dusk spread across the yard. At the chain link fence, where the jasmine grew thick and twisted, fireflies blinked and disappeared. The mulberry tree, a lone silhouette, stretched its limbs toward the night. She climbed into it, found the crook in the middle where the branches split, and curled her body into that nook as if she were an egg in a nest. The usual shadows gathered at the edges of the backyard. The world hummed in quiet tones but Ivy did not feel quiet.

Her father was disappearing. His eyes were sinking deeper into his skull, like there was something inside his head that he needed to get a better look at. His cheeks stuck out at severe angles. His ribs were no more than a cage, his breath shallow and rumbling. When had this trouble started? She tried to trace it back.

He had nibbled his way through the holidays, sometimes complaining of a deep pain in his belly and growing nauseated at the food smells that filled the house. At first, he'd joked about his wife's second-rate cooking skills and followed every meal with a glass of water mixed with a teaspoon of baking soda. Ruby shrugged it off. She got them all fed, day after day, and that was something. She'd never learned to cook anything beyond the realm of boxed and frozen food, never reasoned why she should bother cooking from scratch when pre-packaged food was just as tasty and much more convenient.

By the time spring came, his cheekbones looked as big as his ears, and he'd taken his belt in another notch. The longer Ivy thought about things, the more questions filled her mind. How long is eternity? Is heaven just beyond the horizon, beyond the moon, or in another galaxy? Was a piece of pecan pie heaven to an ant? Was a wide river heaven to a fish?

Her father spent the week in his easy chair, waiting for an opening in the surgeon's busy schedule, knocked out on pain pills that made him sleep through the whole day. Ivy went to school every morning and came home in the afternoon expecting to find him up and about and feeling better, expecting him to come to the supper table and eat. But he never did. Toward the end of the week, her expectations were gone.

On Friday she woke to a hymn playing inside her head. *Just as I am, without one plea.* It was her father's favorite church song. Their congregation sang it all the time, the words implanted in her brain. She couldn't shake the phrase, or ignore it. *Just as I am.* The refrain haunted her all day, in the pause between her teacher's instructions, at lunch when she emptied her tray in the bin, on the way out the door after the bell rang. The song persisted. When school let out, she didn't want to go home. She rode her bike down the dirt path that ran through the field by her house.

Just as I am followed her around the rest of the day, until she stood on the railroad tracks with a notion to make it stop. But the voice inside her head was stubborn, and even as she stood on the tracks, it only grew louder.

Then a siren started in the distance, soft at first, then growing louder. She knew instantly: the ambulance was coming for her father. As she pedaled down the dirt path toward home, a window opened in her mind's eye and she could see what had happened. Time is like that when the world is twisting in on itself and turning upside down. Maybe she was wrong. Maybe it was the old man across the street. He was old and his time was near. Maybe it was him that ambulance was coming for this time.

She stopped at the edge of the yard. Frankie paced back and forth, his hands pressed tight against his ears, his steps quick and nervous. Her father lay sprawled in the grass and Ruby was on her knees next to him. Their dog, Rock, whined and nudged her father's shoulder. The ambulance driver cut the siren, turned into their driveway, and stopped just behind the Oldsmobile.

Ruby glanced up as Ivy approached and said, "Where have you been?" The question flew at the girl like a bat caught inside a barn. She couldn't answer.

Her father's face was paler than his sweat-stained t-shirt. His legs were strewn carelessly, as though they might not still be joined, foot to ankle, leg to hip. Everything about him was damp and clingy, and he smelled of soured sweat.

Ruby wiped his face with a cold towel and said, "Don't you leave me, Hank. Don't you dare."

The attendants lifted him onto the stretcher and into the ambulance. Her mother climbed into the back alongside him. She gathered the skirt of her yellow housedress, tucked it under her thigh, and crouched down beside him. "Girl, don't you step one toe outside this yard before I get back," she called to Ivy. "Keep your eye on your brother and don't let that dog chase us."

Ivy caught Frankie's hand in her own and asked, "Is he going to be all right?"

"God's will," Ruby said.

Ivy knew about God's will. A vision of it formed in her mind: ancient letters printed on a parchment scroll wrapped around ornate gold handles and carried on a cloud so that it should never touch the earth. There was no way to know God's will. She stared into the back of the ambulance, at the stretcher, the blinking machines, the soles of her father's socks. She gripped Frankie's fidgeting hand tighter with her right hand, curled her fingers around Rock's collar with her left and said, "Stay."

The driver slammed the rear double doors shut and said, "Don't worry, kid. We'll take good care of your pop." Tires crunched over gravel and the ambulance backed slowly out of the driveway. She swallowed the panic threatening to bust up through her lungs.

Frankie craned his neck, watching until the ambulance was out of sight. When it turned off their street, the siren sounded again, screamed for a moment, and then faded in the distance. He looked at the corner where it disappeared, brought a fingernail to his mouth and started chewing.

Ivy stared at the three small maple trees that her father had planted next to the driveway the year before. He'd planted one for each of them, his wife, son, and daughter, but he hadn't planted one for himself. It was something Ivy had pestered him about. They were a foursome and she considered the planting incomplete.

"Come on, Frankie," she said. They walked through the front door. The bottle of pills sat on the kitchen table. She put them in her pocket and led Frankie out the back door to the backyard. Everything was in its place: the bass boat, the tool shed, the rusted oil drum pushed against the house, the mulberry tree. Being left in charge of her brother calmed her. She wiped her nose with her sleeve and pulled herself up into the tree.

Beneath her, Frankie turned his radio on and held it to his ear. Ivy would've liked to talk to him but a baseball game was in progress and he would be lost to it for several hours. Her thoughts turned dark like a cloud pooling into itself and deepening. A daddy longlegs climbed onto her hand from the trunk of the tree and she was glad for the company. It crawled from one hand to the other on stick legs that tickled her skin. She held her hand flat against the tree and it climbed back onto the trunk.

The next afternoon, they went to the hospital to visit her father. The buildings sat on a peninsula at the north end of the bay on a shore lined with cattails and live oaks. The trees were bigger than any Ivy had ever seen, branches draped in Spanish moss, thick and gray like old men's beards. A splintered fishing dock leaned over the water, near a small beach. A building near the beach was marked with a sign that read "Sanatorium." Outside it, unshaved men in gray pajamas walked on dirt paths, smoked cigarettes and played checkers. Some of them talked to themselves out loud. Some of them shook their fists and swore at a vacant sky.

Ruby glared at the men and yanked Ivy's arm. "Don't be wandering off, you hear?" and waved her hand at the small, cleared area in front of the hospital. There were a couple of concrete benches for visitors or patients to rest on, and another small building with a sign that read "canteen." Ruby pulled off her sunglasses, bent down and pushed her face into Ivy's. "There's some things you don't understand, you hear me?"

Ivy twisted out of her mother's grasp and rubbed her shoulder. Some things? When had she ever understood anything that was going on?

"Keep Frankie with you," Ruby said. She gave her a dollar and went inside the sick ward to see Hank. Children were not allowed inside the hospital. Ivy gazed out over the small beach. It was, she knew, the same beach where her mother and father had met some umpteen years ago. Ivy remembered the stories of their early courtship. She knew they'd stood right there, on that beach, their pant legs rolled up, their toes covered with sand, mooning over each other with shining eyes.

Ivy walked to the canteen, a small metal building with a rounded roof and a slatted wood porch. The man behind the counter said he was used to kids being dumped there and told her about the fat raccoons that skulked in the palmetto bushes and crept beneath the porch. Bandits, he called them because of their markings and because they prowled around in the dark and stole things out of the dumpster. "They'd steal your last breath," he said.

She bought a package of peanut butter crackers and gave half of them to her brother. Frankie, who was never interested in wildlife, pressed his radio to his ear and paced the dirt path that ran alongside the building where her father was housed.

A few minutes later, an attendant pushed Hank outside in a wheelchair so wide it nearly swallowed him. Ruby was at his side. "He can't sit up long," she said. "But he wants to see his children."

They'd wrapped a wool blanket around his shoulders despite the warm afternoon air. Stretched-out socks fell loose around his ankles. Ivy's legs felt hot and weak.

Hank touched Ivy's hair, a gesture that was as old as she was. "You got to promise me you'll take care of the two of you now." The words rattled inside his chest.

Ivy stared at his gray pajamas, then off into the woods where the raccoons waited. The doctors, the pills—it was clear that nothing had worked. Her head pounded. She didn't know how to take care of anyone. She wanted him to stay and take care of them all.

Ruby sat nearby on a concrete bench, her legs crossed at the ankles, her hands clutching a damp handkerchief, eyes hidden behind her sunglasses. Frankie stood next to her, poked a finger in the air and said, "Here comes the three-two pitch."

Old men and their nurses gathered at the water's edge to watch the sunset layer itself in shades of cinnamon. Somewhere nearby, Ivy couldn't tell just where, a cricket began its night noise. Hank shivered. He raised his arm toward the sky and waved as though he'd seen an old friend. "Yes, yes. I'm coming," he said to the sky.

Ivy imagined the hand of Moses reaching down through the clouds. Maybe it was the pain that made him talk like that. Maybe it was the buckets of medicine they'd pumped into his body. Maybe sickness had granted him some kind of vision.

"What's over there?" Ivy looked at the sunset, half-expecting heaven's chariot to swing low, right out of the orange sky, to carry him home.

He smiled and lifted his chin to the light in the melting sky. Ivy saw a shimmer in the air around her father and heard the cricket's song. The last bit of orange vanished into the horizon. A flock of pelicans flew past in single-line formation, skimming the water with their wing tips, and the crowd of old men outside the sanatorium applauded. As night chill drifted in from the bay, the attendant wheeled Hank back inside.

"Stay with Frankie," Ruby said as the door swung shut behind her.

There are people who swear by the knowledge given to them in the night. In her last years, Ivy's old grandmother had always declared that her dead husband visited at regular intervals to tell her when the hot water heater had a leak or the car needed an oil change. Ivy had watched her mother raise an eyebrow at these stories, and felt the same suspicion. Yet the next morning it was a dream that brought her the news. She'd seen him walking down a red clay road with a crowd of strangers. As soon as she opened her eyes, she'd known he was dead.

In the half-light of waking, she imagined his body, small and broken, slung in a heap on the ground, dust gathering in the crevices of his face. Her brain turned white and noisy. Her eyes darted around her bedroom, seeing everything, settling on nothing. Outside, a raven landed on the mulberry tree and cracked the air with a screech. It fought a sudden gust, spread its wings and flew away. Ivy imagined herself rising into the wind, her bones hollow and airy. She moved through the house staying low to the ground, holding onto doorknobs, touching the thick walls, all the solid things that might not come undone.

Wind caught the back door and it slammed open. The sky, there was no end to it, so big it could suck her into space. She ran to the mulberry tree and settled in the crook of its trunk, wrapped her arms around the thickest limb. Her hair whipped at her eyes but she closed them and clung to the tree until the wind lessened and heavy rain moved in from the gulf.

It rained for two days, so heavily that even at midday the world seemed gray. The sun refused to show itself and Ivy imagined it had drowned somewhere across the ocean. She slept not knowing when she was dreaming or waking. She floated through time, anchored to nothing and no one, watching people come and go—ladies from the neighborhood, a man with papers for Ruby to sign, another who wanted to pick up her father's burial clothes. Ivy stared at things, the food she couldn't bring herself to swallow, hollow laughing characters on the television, her hands. She drank chocolate milk, sure that solid food would make her ill. On the morning of the third day, they buried her father.

Funerals were unknown territory. All Ivy knew about them was what she'd learned on television after President Kennedy was shot. On that day, they'd let school out early and when she got home, her father and mother were sitting on the sofa watching Walter Cronkite, his voice breaking as he struggled to find the comforting words for a broken nation.

"The President's been shot!" Frankie had said. They'd sat in front of the television, the four of them, spellbound by the impossible. The president was dead.

Ruby hadn't watched the coverage of the days that followed. Displaying Mrs. Kennedy's grief for the whole world to see was, she said, in poor taste. And then Oswald was shot. Ruby said she didn't want to think about how crazy the world was getting and had spent the day outside pulling sandspurs out of the yard.

The horse-drawn carriage, the family dressed in shades of gray and black. Ivy had watched the funeral while holding her father's hand. If he were here now, he would hold her hand. But he wasn't.

Ruby had been holed up in her bedroom through the days of rain, gravity and grief pinning her to the mattress. Church women brought casseroles for Ivy and Frankie. Ivy watched them move through the house, their eyes empty, their faces frozen and blank, trying to get Ruby out of bed and dressed. They seemed like robots, cooking and cleaning, and talking in monotone voices, gutless, bloodless, life-sized dolls moving silently around her.

Ivy found his bottle of pills on the table next to his easy chair. She carried them to her room and bundled them inside his old sweatshirt that she'd hidden on the floor of her closet. She put on a wrinkled skirt and blouse and sat in his easy chair, staring at her shoes, until it was time for the service.

The church was filled with people and the too-sweet smell of lilies. Rain blocked the light from the windows. Ivy's skin crawled at the sight of the casket and the spray of flowers draped across the top. She couldn't stand the thought of him being in there. Her arms and legs tingled. Her vision wavered until she didn't feel a part of this world anymore.

The sky opened up with a rain so thick and gray she thought it might never stop. From the backseat of the car, she and Frankie watched them lower the casket into the ground. Her father, stiff and cold in the ground. For once Frankie wasn't listening to his radio. Tiny hairs had sprouted on his upper lip and chin. He wore their father's Sunday jacket, though it was too big for his narrow shoulders.

Back at their house, people crowded through the front door, shaking their umbrellas, dripping rain. The place was too small for all these people and Ivy wanted them gone. Her bedroom was the depository for the stuff they carried, her bed a puddle of purses and wet coats. She picked them up, dumped them in the hallway, and locked her bedroom door behind her. There were only five pills left in the bottle. She swallowed them, hoping they would be enough, and climbed inside his old sweatshirt, pulling the hood over her head like a cocoon. She stretched out on the cold floor, hidden in the narrow space between her bed and the wall, and slept, stiff as a corpse, trying to understand the world of the dead. The floor rolled beneath her like a giant wave that held her aloft.

Sometime during the night, a thunderstorm swept through and rocked the sky. The ceiling of her room split open. Thunder cracked and she grabbed hold of it, rode it above the storm, watching the night dissolve beneath her. The star-filled universe was open to her now. She soared through it, looking for signs and sounds of him, hoping to find where he had gone.

There was static in the air that slowly turned into music she recognized. Frankie was pacing in the hallway outside her door with the radio pressed against his ear.

He tapped on her door. "Trix are for kids," he said, which meant she should get up and fix his breakfast.

She might have floated through the skies while she was passed out on her Dad's leftover pills, might've even sensed his presence somewhere out there for a moment. But she was back in her old room, groggy and thick-headed. She tested her fingers, clenched her fists, willed her eyes to open. The white walls of her bedroom came into focus, the faded pink curtains that needed washing, the ceiling solid and intact. The cold floor sent a chill up her spine that cleared her head a bit. She peeled off her dad's old sweatshirt as morning light fell all around her.

Not So Fast

Bristol sat in her bed looking through the photographs a classmate had taken of her for an interview that was scheduled for later that night. Like most nights, her roommate Caden had gone to bed after their allotted two hours of streaming. The girl was sound asleep but now she cried out. It happened every night. Sometimes she let out a small yelp, sometimes it was full-blown wailing. Both were heartbreaking. Bristol waited to see if Caden would quiet but when the moaning began, she reached across the space between their narrow beds and squeezed the girl's hand. Caden stopped crying and Bristol, having defeated the nightmare one more time, felt the knot in her own stomach relax.

Each night it was the same. She and Caden had shared a room since Caden was twelve and Bristol was thirteen years old. Caden was especially troubled the first year and always whimpered after she fell asleep. Almost every night back then, Bristol would wake to find Caden in bed next to her. They'd both been taken from their mothers in an operation run by county law to flatten the uptick in opioid use that was spreading across the state, and foster care homes popped up all over Biggs County. Six kids to a house, sometimes seven. Bristol knew right away that this was intended to be a long-term situation; her own mother got seven years for selling. It had been five years and she'd never even heard when or if the woman got out.

All the girls in Bristol's house missed their mothers, some more than others. Nightmares occurred throughout the house routinely, and Bristol typically stayed up at least until midnight, knowing that even if Caden was okay, another girl down the hall would need her. It became her role to soothe them, as the staff took the stance that given time each girl would eventually grow out of it and ignored them. Bristol being the oldest in her house, the girls looked to her to figure things out. Even the simplest things were left to her—which boy band was the hottest, whether chocolate ice cream was better than vanilla. If one of the girls got a scratch, they'd cry until Bristol appraised the damage and applied a bandage. If a lightning storm washed across the sky, they'd all crawl under Bristol's bed. At first, it gave her a sense of importance, a sense she belonged. She had the power to comfort, to decide.

Three staffers ran the house and another took the weekends, but over the years everyone had just gotten used to checking with Bristol. The weekend house manager would not even start supper until Bristol had given the approval for the night's meal. Pizza or burgers? Cookies or cupcakes? The same questions, every Friday and Saturday night. No one ever made a decision without her approval.

While the girls watched the Disney channel after supper, Bristol helped hand out the bedtime meds. The smaller ones didn't put up such a fuss if the meds were handed out halfway through dessert. Ice cream made life easier in the house, no matter if every one of them was getting pudgier by the month. Bristol was washing and drying their bowls when she noticed that the medicine cabinet had been left unlocked. She pulled it open and read the prescriptions. Xanax, in various strengths, for each girl. How many years would it be before the state cracked down on benzodiazepines? The kids that survived foster care would leave addicted. They'd score some menial job that might keep them fed but they'd be looking for dope on the street. The county would sweep out the dealers, another generation would enter the system, and the contract with the pharmaceutical industry would be renewed. Take a kid's parents from them and turn them into an addict.

The odds were stacked against them but there had to be some way out.

The bottle with her own name on it was different than the others but she wasn't surprised. Early on the docs had said she was hyperactive, and then another changed her diagnosis to depression. At the hospital she'd heard personality disorder whispered behind her back but to her face they called it a mood disorder. All she knew was that she was sad. She thought she had a right to be.

She'd been spitting out her pills for three days now and could feel the familiar distortion settling in behind her eyes. She'd learned that sort of thing got unwanted attention from the staff and hid it well. Coming off the stuff was hard and she'd been involuntarily admitted three times in the last two years, but she had to try one last time to get clean. She was glad it was the weekend because she wouldn't have to deal with the nosy teachers at her high school. They were always watching her. Last week, just laughing too loud in chem lab got her sent to the school social worker. But she was graduating in a month. All she wanted was her freedom.

The house manager came down the hall for her nightly rounds, checking that each girl was in her assigned bed. She opened the door briefly, looked at Bristol and the sleeping Caden, and turned off their overhead light. Bristol went to the window, slid the curtains to the side, opened the window. The scent of late-blooming jasmine and yellow moonlight filled the room. A breeze stirred the air.

Caden rolled over and opened her eyes. "Don't go."

"I have an interview." Bristol slipped on her jeans and unzipped her backpack. She reached under her mattress for an envelope.

Caden threw back her sheet. "You mean an audition. At the club?" Caden grabbed the envelope and pulled out a photo of Bristol, her naked back to the camera.

"Call it what you want." Bristol stood with her hand out, waiting. They both knew Caden would give it back and that once Bristol was gone, Caden would cover her absence.

A car engine idled on the street two houses down. Bristol pulled her dark hair into a ponytail.

Caden leaned out the window to see the car. "You know there will be drunk men there, right? And they'll be pawing at you."

"I know it pays good money. Better than Walmart or Waffle House. And it's a lot easier to dance your way through life than it is to sling pancakes."

Caden handed the photo back.

"I'll be eighteen next week, Caden. How long do you think they'll let me stay here? I got to have my own money to start out on my own."

"You should talk to your case manager. Maybe you can work here."

"They won't let me. You know they got a hard-on over that fucking mood disorder shit. Now Walmart won't even consider my application, what with the number of times I've been admitted."

Caden dropped back down on her bed. "Are you coming back tonight? The little girls are planning a birthday party for you. It'll crush them if you ruin their party."

"I know. Jeez, all week it's been like streamers or confetti, picnic or Chinese buffet? You'd think no one ever had a birthday before."

"It's all they have to look forward to. And they're all worried that when you move out, they'll never see you again."

"I can't help that. I never wanted to live here, never wanted a bunch of crybaby girls hanging off me."

Caden turned her head into her pillow and Bristol knew she had hit a nerve. Good, if that's what it took to get a little space. She planned on getting back to the home unnoticed by sunrise. She and Caden could make up.

She crawled out the window.

The passenger side door of the Jaguar was unlocked. Bristol glanced toward the backseat to make sure the woman was alone before getting in.

"You ready for this?"

"Yeah, I'm ready."

"I only ask because you aren't wearing what I told you to. Where's that slinky top?"

Bristol's head spun a little with the worry that the woman would tell her to get out. That, and the fact she hadn't taken her pills for a few days. She pulled a pink satin top from the bottom of her backpack.

"I've got it. I'll change on the way." The woman smiled and reached over to take the tie out of Bristol's hair. "You're prettier with your hair down."

It wasn't the first time the woman had touched Bristol but it was just as much of a thrill. Bristol made herself lean into the seatback and not look at the woman. She was beautiful and if she thought Bristol was hot, then it might actually be true. They rode over the bay-way bridges with the windows down, the warm breeze on their skin.

The woman laid her hand on Bristol's knee and it felt like lightning shooting straight to her core. For a moment she froze, wondering if the woman would slide her hand up her thigh, but she didn't. Bristol wrapped her fingers around the woman's hand.

It was the wrong move. The woman pulled her hand back and put it on the steering wheel.

"No one is going to hold your hand tonight. You know that, right? We're not going to prom."

"I know that," Bristol said. She felt the sudden impulse to jump out of the car.

The woman laughed. "Put that top on. We're almost there and I don't want to keep anyone waiting."

The car slowed for a turn onto a gravel road. Bristol pulled her t-shirt over her head.

"I thought we were going to the casino."

"I said it was a high-end party. I didn't say a casino. If things go okay, we can talk about the casino next time."

"Is it just a house?"

"Trust me kid, this is not just a house."

The woman turned onto an oyster shell road that seemed a mile long. A half-moon cast shadows through the palm trees and oleanders that lined the drive. The house came into view when they rounded the last bend, three stories high and as wide as a strip mall. Sportscars of obscure brands that Bristol had never seen before were parked in front, along with three limousines.

A chill went up the back of Bristol's arms. Even on a warm night like this she would freeze in the little top she had brought. She tried to think of a harmless question that wouldn't anger the woman, one that wouldn't trigger her warning system. She thought of her case manager, the high school social worker, and the house staff.

"How do you know these people?" she said.

The woman slipped her finger beneath Bristol's black bra strap.

"Don't worry about it. You won't know anyone. Do this for me and everyone gets along just fine."

The woman took Bristol's hair, wrapped it in her fist, and pulled her close. Bristol had been kissed before but this kiss shook her. She felt a new kind of tension down her spine, through her crotch. The woman tightened her fist around Bristol's hair and pulled her closer. Bristol couldn't have turned away if she'd wanted to, but no part of her body wanted this to end. She wanted the woman to touch her everywhere. Briefly Bristol wondered if she was queer. Maybe she'd been queer all along. Maybe that was the problem with her this whole time. Maybe that was why she didn't fit in. The only thing she knew for sure was that, whatever the night was about to throw at her, she wanted to be beside the woman. But then the woman pulled back.

"Put the top on. Don't forget your backpack."

They got out of the car. The walkway to the house was lit with torches that flickered so maniacally that Bristol wondered if they were real or only in her head. In the distance the night pulsed with the beat of a disco.

Two men wearing Polo shirts and oversized red ballcaps walked out of the house. The woman's phone binged and she stopped.

"I'll be right there," the woman said. "Listen, they'll ask you to do a lot of different things, but if you say no, they'll back away. You also won't get paid. Your choice."

One of the men, the one in the pink Polo shirt, took her elbow. "Follow me."

"Give me a minute," the woman said and waved at the air before turning to answer her phone. When she reached the front door, Bristol glanced back and saw the woman's car start down the driveway. Bristol started to turn around, but pink Polo dude had a grip on her arm.

"Don't worry," he said. "She's just going to pick up another candidate. Lots of girls want this gig, you know?"

The first floor was an enormous room with couches and loveseats, marble floors, and floor-to-ceiling windows on the opposite wall. Dozens of men sipped drinks from sparkling glasses. When Bristol entered the room, each of them scanned her head to toe. An electric current ripped at the back of her head and the room wobbled. The guy at her elbow kept her walking and the men returned to their conversations. She wondered if she'd already been passed over. They exited through a wall of sliding glass doors that led to a lawn sloping down to an oversized swimming pool with several inflated white swans and clumps of water lilies.

Music blared through speakers set up along the perimeter of the yard. A DJ danced behind a table set up high above the far side of the pool. A hundred half-naked people danced in the grass around the pool but no one was in the water. A breeze washed across the surface of the pool and ruffled the lily pads. A girl wearing only panties stood on the diving board, searching the water below her, her thin arms folded protectively over her breasts.

"If she doesn't do it, it'll be your chance." Pink polo dude relaxed his grip on Bristol's arm.

The DJ cut the music and the crowd quieted. Men from inside lined the veranda. A spotlight lit the girl on the diving board. She covered her mouth with her hand as she stared into the water.

The guy pulled Bristol through the crowd to the edge of the pool.

"Will she do it?" the DJ asked, and the crowd yelled, "Jump."

The girl laughed nervously. She pointed into the pool and Bristol followed the line of her arm. An alligator sat on the bottom of the pool just below the girl.

"What the fuck?" Bristol stepped away from the edge of the pool, but the guy caught her arm again.

"Take it easy. It's only a four-footer. The magnification of the water makes it seem bigger than it really is."

"She's supposed to jump in there with it? That's fucked up."

"She has a choice."

The girl leaned over the water so far that Bristol thought she might fall in.

"Is she high?"

"Hah! No, she's broke." The guy didn't even look at Bristol. "She gets a thousand for every gator she outswims."

The girl sat down on the edge of the board and stirred the water with her foot. Behind her the lily pads rustled and the ridged spine of another alligator quietly broke the water's surface as it floated into view.

"Careful!" someone in the crowd yelled and the girl tucked her foot underneath her thigh.

The gator swam under the board. It was smaller than the one sitting on the pool's bottom but now the girl chances were cut in half.

"This is whacked," Bristol said.

"Nah. It's just a little fun. Almost anyone can outswim little gators like those. Besides, that girl is dumb as a rock. How else is she going to make money? I mean, look at her. Skinny little fuck, no tits. Girls like that can't even suck a guy off proper."

Bristol tried to jerk her arm away. He flicked his finger at the lace on her top and tightened his grip.

"What'd you think you were coming here for, a fashion show?"

When she was in fifth grade, Bristol's class had taken a field trip to a gator farm, where a man dangled dead chickens over the water. The bigger ones could jump ten feet out of the water if they were hungry enough. Even though the two in the pool were smaller, Bristol was too close to the water if either of them was starving.

"I didn't come here for this." She tried to pry his fingers off.

"Easy there, girl. You came here of your own accord to entertain the party. Your pal in the Jag already got her cut. You'll get paid if you swim fast enough. Just think what you can buy with that money."

The girl on the board waved a finger no, stepped off the board, and ran back to the deck. The crowd moaned and shouted for her to come back, but another gator had floated into view and the girl refused.

"Good thing for you she chickened out," the guy said and dragged Bristol toward the diving board. "Here's what you do. Go out to the end of the board and tease the crowd. Make a big deal of being scared."

"But I am scared. I'm not diving into that pool."

"Once you get out there, take off your top and show them what little bit you've got. Make it a tease. Then take off your jeans, they'll only slow you down in the water."

He kept his grip on her arm and pushed her up on the board. The crowd got loud again.

The guy smiled. "I feed them every few days. I doubt they're all that hungry."

She tried to pull away again and he yanked her toward him.

"Stop fucking around. These people came for a show and you're going to give it to them. Just dive straight toward the swim out."

Another gator appeared from beneath the lily pads.

"There's another thousand for you right there."

She could buy all the girls at home new bikes and take them all out for supper.

"How many are there?"

"Doesn't matter. You get paid for how many I see when you dive. I see five. Where else you going to get five grand for one minute of work? Get going."

At the other end of the pool, the woman reappeared with another girl at her side. Another man held that girl's wrist. The woman smiled at Bristol and cocked her head as if to say, "What'd you expect?"

What had she expected? A party? Here it was. To get noticed and feel like a rockstar? This was her chance.

All her life she'd been swimming in rivers and lakes, knowing there were gators lurking on the mucky bottom, invisible and shrouded in the weeds and mud. She studied the water. Now there were six. What were six half-grown gators swimming lazily in a clear pool? Everyone was watching her, chanting for her to jump. She calculated the distance to the swim-out and guessed it to be twenty feet.

"Six thousand," she yelled to the guy.

He pulled out a wad of cash and held it up for her to see.

She stepped to the very end of the board, felt it lift and fall beneath her feet. She pulled her top over her head and the crowd screamed louder. She unzipped her jeans, stood on one foot and then the other, got them off without falling in. The crowd was a low murmur now, just a buzz inside her head.

The gators gathered below the board. They would fight for whatever prize they got and she knew she could be ripped apart before she even bled out. She rolled her jeans into a ball, tied them together with the pink top.

She looked at the guy again. What was he thinking? That these people wanted to see a girl torn limb from limb, to see the water turn red with her blood? Maybe they did. Maybe she wouldn't even be the first.

She backed up on the board and threw her balled-up clothes at the middle of the clump of gators. Instantly they attacked it. She ran down the board and dove to the swim-out. Two kicks in the water and she was at the edge, climbing out. She rolled away from the pool and the crowd surrounded her, pulling her to her feet. They were laughing and pointing at something in the water.

Two of the gators tore at her jeans, ripping them in half at the crotch and dragging the legs to the bottom. Another one had shredded the top. Pink strips of fabric were caught in its teeth. It didn't matter. She had been faster than them and now she wanted to get out of there, crawl back through the bedroom window and show the cash to Caden. In the morning she could take the girls out to breakfast, maybe even spurge on an afternoon at the movies.

The guy came over, laughing and holding the cash above his head. Bristol reached for it but he pulled his hand away. The crowd yelled for more.

"Huh-uh, little girl. Not so fast." He dangled the money over the water. "Do it again."

The Train Runner

The girl with the straw-colored hair stands on the railroad track, sunlight glaring, bouncing off the metal rails, sparkling against the flint in the fill rock. She rubs the top of her head to soothe the heat building there, wishes she owned a ball cap to protect her burning scalp. The four o'clock train is due. Push her for words and she'll say the thundering train thrills her to the bone, or that she has no fear.

She's dressed in her father's threadbare work shirt, the only remnant of him after he left for the war, and hand-me-down shorts, frayed at the cuffs, but with deep pockets where she can keep a coin. Her dog, still plump with puppy fat, has taken to following her through the afternoon hours after school lets out. He sits on the track, scratching at his ear. Reaching down to tighten a shoelace, she wonders if the train will be on time, though it always is.

Shielding her eyes with a salute of sorts, she looks up the track, trying to see beyond the bend. It's obscured by a stand of reforested pine. With her right foot resting lightly on the steel rail, she feels for a vibration. For a moment she imagines herself an army scout listening for enemy invasion. Sensing the softest rumbling, she sighs with satisfaction, for her skill is sharpening every day. She pulls the coin from her pocket, spits on it and places it in the center of the rail.

A plume of white smoke lifts over the tree line. At the first sight of the black iron grille coming around the bend, the girl and dog run into the shallow ravine and crouch. Maybe this time the coin will withstand the shuddering quake of the engine and be flattened to perfection.

The train lunges closer. The conductor leans out the window, sees the girl and tugs hard on the whistle pull. A screeching wind booms down the gully.

But smashed coins are useless. The candy aisle at the commissary, its bins of bubblegum, caramels, and chocolates, will be lost to her. She leaps out of the broad ditch and runs toward the track to grab the coin that would open the door to a sugary afternoon. It's a trick she's done before. The dog stands, the fur along his spine stiffens. He wants to follow her but the train is bearing down now, billowing steam and a deafening roar.

She reaches the coin, snags it with her fingertips and rolls it into the palm of her hand, then darts across the track to the opposite ravine. The windblast from the speeding train whips the shirt against her skin and pins her to the ground. Her heart pounds in her chest. Her lungs heave and contract. Blood pulses in her temples, floods her brain, rushes through her limbs. She feels it in every muscle, even in her marrow, this youthful, fatal notion that she will live forever.

Rising

Elise stuffed her carry-on in the overhead bin and found her seat in the back of the plane. Her old habit of thinking she was lucky brightened for a moment when she saw half the plane was empty. But she had long ago stopped thinking of herself as lucky.

The flight attendant came down the aisle writing down drink orders. "Quieres algo de tomar?"

"What?"

"Sorry. We'll be taking off soon. Will you want something to drink once we're in the air?"

She was chubbier and younger than Elise expected for a flight attendant. "Chardonnay, if you have it."

"Pinot Grigio okay?"

It wasn't okay but there was nothing to do about it. Elise nodded.

"Please bring your chair upright for the takeoff." The attendant wrote down the order, handed Elise a pack of peanuts, and moved up the aisle. Elise wondered how much of the world the flight attendant had traveled. The question made Elise envious. No doubt more than herself. She hoped no one would take the seats on her row, but the doors were closing now and she felt lucky again. She'd be able to stretch out for the overnight flight to Lima.

It's just an adventure. She deserved some time on her own. How many times had she told herself that? Leaving the house, in the taxi, at the airport bar, waiting for her plane to board. Now that it was too late to exit the plane, the line she told herself changed. She was being selfish. Once the plane landed, instead of traveling on to Cusco City, she should just turn around and go back home.

The plane backed away from the gate. Lights brightened the runway. In another moment the plane was gathering speed, the force of it pressing her into her chair. The lift alarmed her. It seemed abrupt and too steep, but in a few more seconds it began to level out. Below her, city lights outlined the interstate and neighborhoods of her home town. The plane banked sharply and headed south, over water, into darkness. She'd never flown alone before and here she was going to a foreign land. It was exhilarating. And scary as hell. She picked at the chipped paint on her fingernails, dug through her pack and found her travel bottle of polish remover.

It took the flight attendant fifteen minutes to bring the wine, so Elise ordered two more bottles, and got out her credit card.

The attendant waved it off. "It's okay. I have a few coupons."

There she was, lucky again. She wondered if it was a sign that the universe approved of this trip.

She'd chosen Peru for the puma, the black cat that hunted the jungles of the Andes Mountains, because that was a trip that she felt sure she could sell to her husband and kids. They had humored her over the summer while she spent hours volunteering at a local big cat rescue. She cleaned cages for bobcats, tigers and one ancient puma that never looked her in the eye but slapped its tail on the ground when she stood outside its cage. In the end her husband went along with her sudden devotion to pumas. By fall she had convinced herself that she had to see one of them in the wild. Her daughter, home on college break, looked it up on Google and said as a spirit animal, pumas represented transition, that yeah, maybe it would be good for her to go.

The airfare was an expensive indulgence for a woman with no career to speak of and two kids in college. She'd become her mother-in-law's chauffeur, her personal guide through years of waiting rooms and medical procedures, flipping through travel magazines and making mental lists of where she might go. When the old woman passed, traveling took on a sense of emergency. She could barely fight off the impulse to run. The years of carting the woman around had left her numb and hollowed out. But running around the planet was for young people. And there was the house, the children that came and went from college, and a husband. She tried to assuage the impulse to flee with Internet searches and travel shows. That only made it worse.

The plane leveled out at thirty-thousand feet. She sipped her wine and took out her notebook, a novel she'd meant to read last year, and a bag of almonds. The novel bored her, though, and the almonds were stale. Despite the wine, thoughts rushed in her brain. She wanted to play solitaire on her phone but couldn't figure out how to put it on airplane mode and was embarrassed at her own ignorance. When the flight attendant passed by, Elise held up her phone pathetically. The woman told her it was an extra fifty bucks to use the Internet on board, so Elise opened her photos file instead.

The photos she had used to convince her husband she needed this trip were still in her browser.

"South America has its big three," she'd told him. "The snake, the puma, and the condor. Everything is spiritual there."

"That's nice, honey." But his face was blank. "I don't care if it's a phase. Go, if you want to." He smiled the smile that told her he wasn't interested in talking and she got back to fixing dinner. Later that night, he fell asleep watching baseball. His team won the game but he didn't even seem to notice. That's when she knew he was hollowed out too.

A week later she could barely get out of bed. She looked at the piles of laundry she couldn't find the energy to wash, the gray foam rolling beneath the sofa, the empty refrigerator—and it was clear—this wasn't a phase. She booked the flight.

The plane descended during sunrise. The change in pressure deafened her for a few moments. The flight attendant came through the cabin. Elise put her seat upright. They were almost on the ground and going too fast. How crazy would it be, how exotic, if she made the local news by dying in a plane crash in Peru? The wheels hit the runway hard and the plane bounced, the engines roared. Her heart pounded, the plane slowed and coasted to the gate.

Hundreds of people had gathered in the Lima airport to greet arriving family members. She traded currency, only possible because the woman in line behind her spoke both Spanish and English. She found the Starbucks and got a coffee and bagel by pointing at the menu and uttering a few nouns. When she got to the gate for her connecting flight, they were closing the doors but the pilot was late too, and they let her board with him.

Two hours later she arrived in Cusco City.

A small group argued with a guide at the luggage terminal. He was upset that only six tourists had made it because one couple had missed the flight from Germany. She gathered that it was a bird-watching group and there was an open spot she could take if she wanted. Seven, he said, was enough to make it worth his time. They were headed north, into the Sacred Valley and the Andes Mountains. All retired, German-speaking couples on a hummingbird tour. She would have solitude by virtue of speaking only English.

When she asked about a puma, the guide laughed.

"Maybe yes." He shook his head. "Probably no," he said, as the van drove out of the city. Still, she noticed he had a tattoo of the cat on his forearm. She sat in the back, unhappy with the smell of diesel fumes, listening to the German couples chattering in a language she'd never heard before, content at not having to explain herself.

Peru was dustier than she expected. The road twisted and climbed a few miles, then turned into a two-lane highway cutting through miles of brown fields. The mountains in the distance appeared like sleeping gods. At times they seemed close enough to touch, they had to be hundreds of miles away.

The whine of the engine lulled her, she refused to close her eyes even for a minute. The air was thin and cold and seemed brand new.

They stopped at a roadside tourist restaurant for lunch. The dirt parking lot was enormous with three travel buses parked at the edge and a hundred American tourists inside. A band of dark-haired Peruvian men sang Beatles songs accompanied by flutes and a guitar. It wasn't what she'd expected to find so far from home. Hearing so many people speaking English made her lonely. Couples and families. She should have insisted her husband come with her, or her daughter. She skipped the hot/cold buffet when she saw that the rear of the restaurant opened out to a large yard that sloped down to a river. Two alpacas were tethered on a lawn on the lower terrace, watched over by a teenage boy wearing a red and white poncho and jeans. She wondered if he really dressed that way when he asked if she wanted a photo with him then realized photos with tourists was how he made money.

The alpacas nibbled at the grass at the roots of a tree with such ambivalence in their eyes she decided to keep her distance. She hadn't come all this way to be spit at or bitten. That's exactly what she would do if someone had tethered her to a stake for photo-ops.

The river was broad and quiet, lined with thousands of smooth stones. The air was exquisitely cold by the water, the smell of its minerals drawing her down to its bank. She stood at the river's edge. The water rippled over child-size boulders that led to the opposite shore where a field opened before an ancient ruin. She wanted to cry. She could die here and that would be all right. If she let herself, she could lay down right in the dirt and sob. When had the smell of dirt and water become so foreign? This was what she'd come here for and she wanted to lock the image in her heart forever. That she could still respond so intensely to beauty surprised her.

The boy yelled and scrambled over the rocks down to her. He grabbed her sleeve. "Venga, venga," and she followed him up the river's bank. At the top, he pointed down to where she'd been standing. A slender, spotted brown snake lay coiled between two rocks.

"La serpiente." The boy laughed, throwing pebbles at the snake until one landed, and it slid into the river. He went back to his alpacas and she watched the snake drift downstream in the current. It began to drizzle and she pulled out the small black umbrella she'd packed at the last minute.

"You are *especial*," the guide told her later. "No one on my tours ever sees snakes. Birds only," he said and turned back to the Germans.

She should have kept the sighting to herself. She'd been told all her life what a special girl she was. What had that led to? She'd lost so much already. Her kids had left home, her parents were aging, her eyesight kept her from reading the novels she loved, her hands were too stiff to knit the scarves she used to make for gifts. Each year she felt she was further away from the things she had been promised as a child. Romance, undying love, adventure. Nothing had turned out the way she expected. Every morning when she woke up, her first thought was to wonder how she'd get through the day without injuring anyone, or herself. She didn't want to be *especial*; she only wanted to survive, maybe with a little grace, hopefully some composure.

The van climbed higher as they drove further into the mountains. Fog surrounded and covered the road. Her fingers were chilled and she knew the cold would settle in her bones by night. They climbed higher. The van pitched at an astounding angle, the engine groaning. Suddenly they were above the fog and the sun was setting. It lit the mountains a brilliant yellow, illuminating the high peaks of the Sacred Valley.

The driver seemed unfazed, shifting into a lower gear.

By the time they got to the camp, it was dark. They unloaded their luggage and she hauled her backpack through the mud to a small tent, regretting she hadn't had the foresight to bring a sleeping bag.

Porters had set up a dining tent and offered them a stew with some objectionable meat. She ate the veggies from it, smiled at the Germans when they laughed, and took a glass of wine when they offered it. The wine didn't mix well with the headache settling behind her eyes. She went to her tent. The coca leaves the guide passed out did nothing to help. He had warned her that the altitude might raise her blood pressure and said it would be a day before she acclimated. She listened to the sounds of the Germans settling in for a night of drinking and hoped they would run out of wine soon. They got drunk and passed out around midnight and then the camp was silent. The waxing moon shined brightly inside her tent. She crawled out the front flap.

Yellow moonlight spread up the mountain side, shining on the ancient path they would walk in the morning. The dull thud behind her eyes was relentless. The air was clean and cold, and every breath felt like a drink of spring water. She needed sleep. Her heart pounded at this altitude. She should at least curl in a blanket and try.

When would she ever be alone in the Andes again? Tomorrow they would visit Machu Picchu with two thousand other people and spend the night in a motel in the little tourist town. They'd eat tacos and guacamole and drink beer.

It should be enough for her. It seemed to be enough for the thousands of pilgrims that came here every year.

She needed more than a carefree afternoon and tourist trinkets from the local market. She had always needed more. Everyone told her so. Even as a child. Amusement parks left her feeling empty. High school prom. The sorority at college. She'd never even settled on a major. It was a constant complaint from her husband in those early years. She was too needy, too demanding. Yet, she felt like she'd spent her life in servitude, apologizing for something she was never quite sure she'd done. It was exhausting. This grief that she'd never been able to pinpoint. She wanted something. Something of her own. Something no one could ever take from her.

What if she died here, a result of a foolish decision? What of it? In the end, it was her mistake to make. This single night belonged to her and her alone.

She picked up her backpack and set out.

The path was steep and difficult and lit only by the rising moon. She walked slowly, picking her way along the rocky path, the only human intrusion the pale shadow at her feet. She might have been Eve, alone on the planet, free of sin. Clouds moved in and covered the moon. Fog tumbled over the high peaks in waves.

As she climbed higher, the air thickened and turned to drizzle. Night turned to ink. The path turned to mud. Her foot slipped and she twisted her wrist when she fell. When she stood, she slipped again and landed on her knees. It was a steep incline, a dead-end of brush and mud with no way forward. Descending would be treacherous. She tried to find a level place to sit and slipped in more mud. She'd never been so filthy and it made her laugh. No one from home would even recognize her now.

It had been stupid to leave the campsite and the guide would probably be angry if he had to search for her. No one in the world knew where she was at this moment and such freedom caught her by surprise. She sat with that thought awhile, then got out her umbrella and decided to wait for dawn. She closed her arms around her knees and laid down. Her mind found its familiar darkness, and she slept, silent as a stone.

A string of short and purposeful exhalations woke her, but when she opened her eyes there was nothing but an earthy smell that she couldn't place.

The guide had laughed when she'd said she wanted to see a puma, but she knew they hunted at night and ranged up to a hundred miles. Something brushed silently against the umbrella. She made herself shrink. Her heart beat in her throat, a wing, a rush. There was safety in insignificance. She became a dot on the landscape, a pebble along an ancient trail. By the time she was fully awake the smell disappeared, and all she could hear was the rain, her own panting, and maybe the padding of paws in a distant swish of leaves.

The sky began to lighten under her umbrella. When she opened her eyes, she doubted her memory. It had only been a dream.

The wind shook her umbrella. The rain stopped, the trees were washed and dripping, and she heard the rustle of feathers. She lifted the umbrella and saw a flock of condors sleeping on the ground nearby. Twenty feet beyond them was the edge of a cliff.

A valley spread out below her. The sky was clear and yellowing at the horizon. Snow covered mountaintops, ragged tree lines, and rock slides, settled now for hundreds of years, strewn down along the valley side--all of it glowed in morning light, all of it fed down to the river. And still, no one knew where she was. She was the bandit of her own life and it thrilled her. She had stolen the most precious things—these moments—and they were all she would ever really own.

More condors unfolded and stood to stretch their wings. She folded the umbrella and stashed it in her pack and smiled, wondering if they had mistaken her as one of their own. Then she wondered what it might be like to be one of them, a soaring thing, forever dwelling between earth and sky.

The first condor stood, strode toward the cliff, and simply walked off the edge. It made her heart thrill, but there was nothing to fear. Their wings were bigger than her entire body. The condor lifted, caught the breeze, and floated out over the valley.

The second one followed. And then the next, until each of them spiraled upward on the current.

She watched them until they became black specks against the brilliant blue, until she blinked and could no longer see them, as though they had never been.

At once the sky seemed to both hold her up and pin her to the ground. In that moment she saw herself to be a small thing-- a constantly beating heart with endless and confused longing in a world spinning with black nights and perpetual sunrises, filled with snakes and rivers, cliffs and valleys, and she knew it was enough just to be alive in this world. It had always been enough.

The End

Acknowledgements

A book like this one only makes it into the world through the work of a constellation of brilliant souls who possess a deep understanding of the vital importance storytelling in a national culture that constantly stands on the edge of its own moral precipice.

First thanks go to Bronzeville Books: Danny Gardner who brings a vision of inclusivity and excellence to a publishing house I'm extremely proud to be a part of, Allison Davis who treated this manuscript with compassion and keen insight, and Erin Mitchell for bringing me into the fold.

Thanks to Naomi Norberg for her final touch. Thanks to Julia Borcherts and Kaye Publicity for sending this book into the world with enthusiasm.

Thanks to Reggie Pulliam for excellent cover design. Thanks to Jim Gleeson for inspired cover art.

Eternal gratitude to Tara Vance, Christine Walz, for not giving up the fight.

Special thanks to Anne-Lise Spitzer and the exceptional team at the Philip Spitzer Literary Agency.

Thank you to my friends and mentors for sage advice and encouragement: Sterling Watson, Kimberly Lojewski, Sandra Gail Lambert, Cheryl Hollon, Rhett Devane, Tricia Booker, and Dr. Flora Zaken-Greenberg. I'm grateful to Tracy Lee Bird for her fine editing and the many five o'clock sessions.

Thanks to Elyse Dinh-McCrillis for her work on Glass. And as always, I'm always thankful for the support and friendship of my hometown team.

And finally, to Lyra, my partner and greatest friend. As ever, I am grateful for your support and company on this journey. You bring light to every darkness.

About the Author

Gale Massey is the author of *The Girl from Blind River* which received a 2018 Florida Book Award. Her work has appeared in Lambda Literary, CutBank, CrimeReads, Sabal, the Tampa Bay Times, Saw Palm, and Tampa Bay Noir. Gale was a Tennessee Williams Scholar at the Sewanee Writers Conference, a fellow at Writers in Paradise, and has served as a panel judge for the Lamdba Literary Awards. Her stories have been nominated for a Pushcart prize in fiction and nonfiction. A native Floridian, she lives in St. Petersburg with her partner.